THE FRENCH WARDROBE

A Novel

A. R. SHAW

Dedicated to my daughter, Kelley
The world is yours.

P resent Day
Seattle, Washington

"Mom?"

"Hi, Brian, I just arrived home. Give me a second." Vivienne fumbled for her keys in the driveway of their home. Her son sounded anxious, which wasn't like him.

"Mom!" he yelled into the receiver. "It's Dad."

"Brian, what's wrong?" Her pulse began to pound. He sounded nearly hysterical, and then she heard more sobbing.

"Brian?"

"There's been an accident. I'm so sorry, Mom! Dad's...dead."

The call from her son, Brian, hit Vivienne like a boulder to the chest. Everything ceased in her world for the briefest of moments as the realization actually became her reality. Before the dreadful news sank in, her knees buckled beneath her and she landed hard on the grayed wooden porch.

She'd walked from the driveway to the front of their Lake

Union, Washington, house while searching for her keys in the dark depths of her purse. She'd just had them in her hand when she closed the car door, but her mind was elsewhere. She barely remembered the drive home.

When the phone vibrated in her hand, the tremor had scared her like a sudden sting from a bee, and she sensed that a harbinger of bad news awaited. Her first instinct had been to pitch the mobile as far as her strength allowed. But then she saw who was calling and felt inane for a second. What mother wouldn't want to talk to her adult son in the middle of the day? She'd answered the call, and her first impression came true—the worst news she could ever imagine.

Brian's speech was *off* right away; there was something wrong immediately. He'd held his voice together until the end, and then he broke down. She was silent, in shock for most of the conversation. *This has to be some morbid joke.* But her son wasn't one for making fun of things, especially over something like this. Still, her mind tried to find a reasonable explanation, some semblance of normal in the horrid travesty her life had suddenly turned into.

Todd couldn't be gone. No. There must be some mistake.

After a moment Brian spoke again. "Mom, I have to go to the morgue to identify his body. I'll call you on my way home."

"I...I want to go, too."

His voice was graved with pain. "Mom, no," he said as if she were crazy. "He wouldn't want you to see him...this way."

"Brian, come and get me—now. I want to...I have to say good-bye to him. I have to. It's what *I* want."

There was a silence, then that dragged out for too long. She knew her son was warring within with what his father would want him to do at this very moment, but she needed to see Todd again, one last time, and if Brian wouldn't take her, she'd call a cab because she didn't think she'd be able to drive that distance through the heavy Seattle traffic this time of day, especially after seeing her husband's mangled body.

"I don't think it's a good idea, but I'll be there in a few minutes to pick you up. Mom, you know he was hit pretty badly? Hit and run, in fact. Bicycle versus speeding car. He never saw it coming. The police said he probably didn't feel anything."

"Hit and run?" She couldn't deal with that now. "I know what you're trying to tell me, son, but I still want to see him one last time. He would do this for me."

"I should call Isabel." The thought just occurred to Brian out of concern for his sister living in Paris, France. "She doesn't know."

Her voice was raw, but she said anyway, "No, don't. Let me tell her. The news should come from her mother."

"I'll be there in twenty minutes," Brian said, and then he ended the call.

Vivienne sat there, stunned. The midmorning sun shone bright through the crimson trees, unusual for a fall day in Seattle. No, the ever-persistent gloom of Seattle's norm should be present on a day when the worst possible event in her life has just taken place.

❧ 2 ❧

E arlier that Day
Seattle, Washington

AFTER THE TRIAL, BRIAN TRIED TO CONTROL HIS TRIUMPHANT grin by placing, rather quickly, a placid one on his face as his father had taught him. He walked through the halls of the King County Courthouse and out to the parking lot.

"Show them you're humble. Don't mark yourself with pride; it will come back to bite you. It always does. I've seen pride take down the best of men," his father taught him.

Ladies' stilettos echoed on the polished granite flooring like chiseling on a mausoleum tomb as they passed him by, a few giving him a look that meant they were available to him whether or not he was married; he need only ask. Brian never did partake, but he didn't mind the gazes. He'd given a few of his own out of appreciation, but he was so in love with his wife, Katherine, he couldn't imagine cheating on her. Not yet anyway.

Perhaps he was too much like his father. He loved the man

and knew that he loved him too, but life with Todd Mathis was hard to bear at times. His mother would agree with him; and just as he'd thought of his mother, Vivienne, his phone made a tone alerting him to a text message coming from her.

"Hi, son. Where's Dad?"

Brian was nearly to his car. *I'm not his babysitter today,* he thought to himself and then chuckled at the very idea of his father *needing* a babysitter. Of all people in this world, no. Todd Mathis *was* the babysitter.

He kept them, all of them, wound up tight, except for perhaps his sister, Isabel. No one controlled her. She rebelled from their father the minute she was born. In some ways, Izzy was too much like their father. What she didn't understand was that Todd loved them all so very much and only wanted what was best for them and to keep them safe from all things that would do them harm, though they clashed over this many times when Brian found himself between the two of them.

Isabel satisfied her need for freedom in Paris, where her father couldn't control her every move, though he did try. He couldn't help himself—she was his little girl, after all.

Brian blew out a frustrated breath with thoughts of Izzy and her father arguing well into the night over her sudden college-major change from prelaw to art restoration, which was truly her calling in the end. She'd gotten her way, but not after a war with the great litigation lawyer of King County, Seattle, Todd Mathis.

They still talked and smiled at one another at family get-togethers. But somehow, after the many arguments, their relationship was damaged in a way that seemed irreversible. Only Brian and his mother could tell the difference.

Of course, their holidays and family get-togethers were fine, but Isabel had put up a shield between them long ago, and any attempt on her father's part to ask her about her career was halted deftly by a smile and a change of subject. She'd never give her father credit for his advice on her career or other important matters, and she made it abundantly clear the advice was never welcomed.

Brian, on the other hand, valued his father's advice and guidance. The man could be tough as nails, but Brian never doubted that his father had his back.

All the criticism he endured growing up was only meant to make him a better man, son, husband, and lawyer. There were times when he pushed him too far, but those challenges, in the end, showed him what he was capable of, and few fathers were willing to needle their sons to the brink so they could see what they're truly made of.

Checking the text again, as Brian slipped behind the wheel of his Fiat, he opted to call his mother rather than fat-finger all the tiny buttons on his phone and end up with something instead of *Heck if I know, Mom* more like *Horse if I low, Mom*. And then she'd be really confused. No, it would be safer and less time consuming just to call her.

"Hi, Mom. No, I don't know where he is. I left the office before he came in this morning. I was held up in court today. We're supposed to meet for lunch when I get back to the office. Sure he's not in there in a meeting or something?"

"His cell phone went to voice mail, and his office manager said he hadn't made it in yet."

Brian pulled his phone away from his ear for a second and checked to see if there were any messages from the old man.

"No, I don't have any texts from him. I'm sure he'll show up. He biked in today, right?"

"Yes, of course."

"Maybe he got held up in traffic. I'll check the garage when I get there. Harry, the parking attendant, keeps his bike in lock-up since the last one was stolen. What do you need him for, Mom? Can I help? He's not due home until later today, right?"

"I don't *need* anything," she said. "He just usually calls or texts around this time every day. I hadn't heard from him. When he shows up, have him send me a note."

"Every day? Still? You guys are weird, Mom. I'm just sayin'." Brian wasn't sure if his father's need to keep watch of his mother every minute of every day was endearing or creepy. His father had some strange controlling habits, but nothing too out there to give notice to the looney bin of a new resident. One of those habits was his overprotective nature toward his mother.

"OK, Mom. Don't worry. I'm sure he's fine. Probably ran into someone at the coffee shop and got caught up in a conversation. He sometimes stops there before heading upstairs to the office." As the excuse came out of his mouth, he knew his mother would never believe that one. His father had friends, but would never string together or listen to anyone else string together more than a dozen words at a given time. He certainly would never let anyone delay him from his duties.

"It's just not like him."

He let out a conciliatory breath in the silence after her statement. It certainly wasn't. Todd Mathis was a slave to a routine he'd developed long ago that involved biking in to his downtown Seattle office from their Lake Union home. "I'll have him call you as soon as I see him. Talk to you later, Mom. Love you. I've got to go."

"Bye, son."

He shut off his phone and started the engine of his car, not certain what he was more concerned about: that his mother was worried that his father hadn't contacted her as he'd done *every* day of their marriage or that his father was so overly protective of his mother that he felt the need to check up on her *every* afternoon.

Then he flashed on an incident as a kid where she'd gone to the grocery store after they'd had an argument. Nothing major—Brian couldn't recall what it was even about—but his mom was miffed and his dad had gone into the den. Then he sprang from his chair when he realized he heard an engine in the garage

7

starting up. Next thing young Brian knew, was his dad was flying out the door and watching with frustration as his mother backed down the driveway and drove down the street.

That was before everyone was required to carry cell phones in the Mathis household. His mom returned later that evening with a lot of groceries, and she hardly made eye contact with his dad. He'd paced the floor the entire time she was gone, which was around two hours. Later that evening, they were both smiling again, and whatever had transpired between them, they'd gotten over it. But the incident always left Brian with a sense that his father just couldn't live without his mother; his love for her was clear to see. He was the strongest man Brian had ever encountered, and yet he was reduced to an insecure mug, wearing holes in the hall carpet, if she wasn't where he needed her to be at all times.

3

P resent
Lake Union, Washington

VIVIENNE MATHIS STARED OUT THE IVORY-LACE-BORDERED window of her home. She'd awoken with a strange feeling that morning, and the perpetual overcast atmosphere of early fall in the Northwest wasn't making her feel any more sorted. A gray mist hung over the lake right out her back door beyond the boat moored at the dock. Though she'd read in the weather report that the fog was supposed to clear by midmorning, she'd had her doubts.

After breakfast, she'd sent Todd off to work as usual, with a kiss, as she stood in the entryway of their home, on tiptoes in her cozy robe. He snapped his bike helmet on as usual, and the clickety-clack of his tires sounded as he wheeled the bike through the doorway.

She closed the door, and like every morning, he paused after exiting and waited to hear her click the deadbolt shut and the beep as she reset the alarm while he put on his gloves and began to head for the bike trail right outside the front of their home.

If she didn't perform the locking ritual, he'd knock on the door and remind her to fasten the deadbolt. "Must keep you safe," he would say, otherwise with a smile, but she knew he meant it as a ritual that, like so many others, must be performed for his own piece of mind.

No one else knew of Todd's needs for constant reassurance except for his family. As a prominent, high-powered Seattle attorney, Todd was known as a tough and ingenious litigator; it was his calling in life. And his list of achievements was impressive to his clients and foreboding to his opponents. Vivienne knew his little idiosyncrasies were a small price to pay for everything he'd done to provide her with a good lifestyle. She loved him and could not imagine life without him, not even for a second.

Then after that morning's hair appointment at the salon, she'd thought she'd missed his text when she walked out into the parking lot after noon. Instead, she'd found he hadn't called or texted her at all. She'd brushed off the oversight without a second thought until she began the drive home. On the way, that nagging feeling rose again, and she wondered why Todd hadn't contacted her as he was prone to do all the days of their marriage.

Even if it was rushed, he at least left her a heart or a smiley-face emoticon. Over the years, they'd become adept at the quick, abbreviated conversations. At first, it was a quick call in the afternoon just to say I love you. She knew he was checking up on her under the guise of love, but that's the way it was with them. Todd would never believe she loved him fully. That was something that she'd gotten over in time.

For him, she suspected it was an insecurity from his tragic childhood that had scarred him and that he'd never gotten over his trust issues. He'd always believed Vivienne was too good for him, and she quit trying to prove otherwise but always remained loyal and constant instead, hoping that would, in time, prove her love for him.

Then cell phones and texting came into their world, and such technology was something that aided Todd's insecure need to reassure himself of her every move. She wasn't surprised when he came home one day with a cell phone that he'd bought just for her. It was equipped, of course, with every tracking device available to *keep her safe.*

She'd smiled and accepted this. Again, she reminded herself that it was a small price to pay for his reassurance. Then instead of calls every afternoon, he began to text her, with an occasional call thrown in.

When emoticons came into play, they found a new language and a way to play together. It became a game. Sometimes, he left her a kiss, and she'd respond with one of her own. Other times, it was a happy dancing character or pudgy cat eating a donut. Whatever the symbol, she would answer within seconds. That was what it was all about. *Are you there for me?* he was saying. *Yes, I am,* she would respond.

Not hearing from him that afternoon was concerning, though at first she thought maybe he was just busy or caught up in court, which happened every now and then, nothing to worry about.

By the time she reached her car, she checked for messages again, finding nothing. So she called him instead. The phone rang but then went to messaging, where his voice commanded directions to leave a purpose for the call.

When she pulled into the driveway, she shut off the engine of her car. *He just forgot. You're being silly; everything is fine, a* voice kept repeating in her consciousness, but everything was too still around her. She couldn't shake a strong sense of foreboding.

The weather prediction was right after all. The sun broke through the clouds. Every leaf on the lawn remained, not even shuddering in the slight breeze. The autumn sky, always overcast in the Pacific Northwest, shown bright overhead. *No, something's very wrong,* she told the voice. She opened the car door, and her dove-gray d'Orsay heels crunched on the gravel drive as she strolled toward the house. Then the clasped phone vibrated in the palm of her hand, and she discovered the source of her premonition. As if on command, the sun hid itself behind the dense clouds once again, matching the dark void in her heart.

❧ 4 ❧

P resent Day
Seattle, Washington

BRIAN HAD JUST PULLED INTO THE DARKENED PARKING GARAGE when his phone lit up with an incoming call from a number he didn't recognize, though the caller ID said *Wash State Patrol*.

"Hello?"

"Mr. Mathis?"

"This is Brian Mathis," he confirmed, and suddenly he knew what the voice would say before he uttered a word. A chill ran through him as the officer explained the accident. How his father never knew what hit him. How his lifeless body had been pinned against a brick wall by a driver who then fled the scene. The witnesses said the speeding car came from out of nowhere, moving erratically. It had happened so fast, the officer was sure his father never felt a thing. "A swift death" is what he'd said, and then he apologized for having to use such descriptive language.

"Did you catch him?"

"Uh, no, but we're reviewing the intersection surveillance cameras. We can usually ID drivers with that equipment. It won't take long. We'll get him. We're working on it as we speak, Mr. Mathis."

"How...did you know to call me?" Brian heard himself ask. Another part of his consciousness was in total shock. He heard the words he spoke but felt he was on some kind of autopilot.

"He had your number in his *first to contact* list on his cell phone."

"OK," Brian said, and let silence fill the void, not knowing what to do next. *Dad's dead?*

The officer said, "Sir, we're going to need you to identify his body at the morgue. Can you come down this afternoon? Of course, you'll need to let the rest of the family know. I'm sure this comes as a blow."

"Um, yeah. The morgue..." Brian could hardly believe this nightmare. His voice was barely audible. "I'll uh, be there in a few hours...You're sure it was him?"

"Well, that's the name that was in his wallet and on his phone, sir. His identification matched his appearance. That's also why we need you to come and confirm his identity."

"Yes. I have to tell my mother. She doesn't know..." his stomach lurched. "Excuse me; I have to go."

"Of course, if you have any questions—" the officer began, but Brian had already ended the conversation. He immediately opened his car door and heaved the contents of his stomach onto the parking garage floor. *This can't be happening.* He sat in the car for a moment to gather his thoughts and to ensure that he could focus on driving in heavy traffic. It's a good thing he didn't start out right away.

Though he didn't expect the strong well of emotion coming to him, grief hit him in relentless waves. He found his breath sucking into his lungs and a crushing pain surrounding his heart. And then it came out like an explosion. "No! Oh my God. No!

Dad! No!" His fists pounded the dashboard in a fury he never knew he was capable of. Heaving large breaths through his lungs, he thought he might be sick again. The phone shook in his hands. He was too upset to tell his mother yet, but he knew he must.

And something else occurred to Brian. Something his father confided in him long ago, but he couldn't go there now. This was an accident, not a murder.

Someone passed nearby his car. Brian was oblivious to the wretched sounds he made as the passerby quickly craned a neck at him in suspicion on his or her hurried way to the elevator of the darkened tomb of the parking garage.

After several minutes, Brian pulled himself together. "Oh, Dad. This will break Mom's heart." He sobbed again, knowing he must make the call. He pounded his forehead against the hard leather of his steering wheel.

Then he dialed.

She answered, "Brian?"

In his softest voice, he began after a pause, "Mom?"

5

July 12, 1987
   King County Courthouse
   Seattle, Washington

"ONE MORE FOR THE TROPHY WALL, EH, TODD? NICE WORK FOR a newbie," Charlie Swenson said as he slapped him on the back and walked past him in the hallway. Todd looked up from his position on the bench at the red-faced man. He'd been trying to get his files in order before he headed back to the office. Charlie had always reminded him of someone who was about to have a heart attack or an anxiety attack or both at the same time due to his persistent red-faced complexion, as if he'd just run up five flights of stairs.

"I wouldn't look at it that way. The oil company had all their documentation. They dotted every i and crossed every t. It's not their fault Mr. Reynolds claimed to have worked on the days they weren't even scheduled to clean those tanks. Sure, the other claimants were exposed to benzene as they claimed, but Reynolds wasn't even on staff at those times. He's a digger as far as we can tell."

"Yeah, too bad for the others though. How many are positive for leukemia now?"

"Only one is officially diagnosed. A father of three." Todd shook his head, knowing leukemia was a death sentence.

"So Reynolds was never exposed?"

"No, not once according to the company's records. Now they're charging Reynolds with fraud, and he has a rap sheet pretty long as it is. He's going to wish he'd never worked for Ashugh Oil."

Charlie let out a long whistle and turned to go but abruptly stopped and asked, "How's the new baby? I hear she's a real looker."

Todd couldn't help but smile at the mention of his new daughter. "She's beautiful. Isabel is doing great. I brought her and Vivienne home last Sunday night. They are both healthy, thank God. I've barely had any sleep either."

"Baby keeping you up?"

"Yes, I mean, no, not really. I just can't stop gawking at her. Seriously, Vivienne has thrown me out of her room several times already. I'm sure all new fathers feel this way."

"No...no," Charlie said. "When Meredith was born, I thought she was the ugliest thing I'd ever seen." He chuckled.

"Oh, come on." Todd laughed at his friend.

"I'm telling you the truth. She came out all red. She looked like a giant squalling beet. I seriously thought there was something wrong with her."

"You are awful, Charlie."

"She's gorgeous now, of course." Charlie looked at his watch. "Hey, congratulations on the new baby. I've got to run."

"OK, see ya, Charlie," Todd waved good-bye and finally shoved the stack of papers he'd been sorting into his briefcase.

6

P resent Day
Seattle, Washington

THE FOLLOWING WEEK, VIVIENNE FOUND HERSELF STANDING under a black umbrella, dressed in a matching hue, weeping between her son and daughter, and surrounded by family, friends, and colleagues of the man known as Todd Mathis as she gazed at the casket hovering above the final resting place of her husband. The man she couldn't imagine she could ever live without was inside that casket.

The last time she'd seen him was at the morgue. His crumpled body lay on the stainless-steel table. His head on a block of wood. His dark-brown hair matted with blood in places. They only pulled the paper sheet down to his neck, but she could still tell it had been broken. He was blue. His body was mangled, and she kissed her fingers and pressed them to his forehead one last time, though his skin was cold to the touch. Brian pulled her back to him. He nodded to the official that it was his father lying there, lifeless.

Todd had always been her rock. Since that dreadful morning, she'd lived in a fog that nothing could penetrate. They'd held the funeral off until Isabel could arrive in from Paris. Brian had picked her up from SeaTac Airport and brought her straight home, where she'd crawled into bed with her mother late that night and had never left her side.

Even though Vivienne knew she wasn't alone with the love of her children present, she would forever feel alone in her soul. She was no longer a whole person, instead only a shell. Todd was everywhere she looked. He existed in the way the furniture was arranged in the living room, the coffee mugs he preferred in the cupboard, and the rug in the entryway they'd bought together because he preferred geometric designs over floral.

She couldn't help herself. She slept with his pillow, and she could still smell him as she held it tight against her and tried to muffle her cries. She expected him home any minute; that they had the wrong man's body in the coffin Brian had picked out for his dad. Even though she'd seen for herself that it was him, her mind kept telling her there must be some mistake.

Or worse, what if she hadn't turned the lock that morning when he expected her to and set the alarm? Would that small delay have kept him alive? If she hadn't given into his neurosis just that once. If only she'd not locked the door, maybe that little delay—that little bit of extra time—would have saved his life. Just enough of a moment for him to have passed the corner before the car flew through the intersection without a care. If only...

She couldn't stop the days of endless "if onlys" from overtaking her. Then the tears would come again, and Vivienne couldn't imagine a time when she would ever heal from Todd's death. Her stomach muscles felt battered from her wretched cries over the past days. *Widows went on, right? How did they?* The grief was unbearable for her.

Thankfully, her daughter planned to stay home for another week. At least she wasn't haunting the five-bedroom house all alone.

After the funeral, everyone came to her home. She found herself surrounded by guests and random dishes of salads and main entrees and was expected to smile and carry on like she did when she and Todd had hosted the many parties they'd had at their home in the past. She only wanted to lie down and slide away into sorrow, holding onto Todd's pillow.

She stood in the living room when her husband's secretary came to her, arms wide with an embrace. She'd always been a steely woman in Vivienne's view. Harsh and clipped on the phone, but that was what was needed to be Todd's assistant. Someone who wasn't afraid to offend at a moment's notice.

"I'm so sorry, Vivienne. I never worked for a better employer. I'll miss him terribly," she said, and then sobbed in a way that made Vivienne feel that *she* needed comfort. But Vivienne herself was the one in need and couldn't give it to anyone else. Hers was all gone. Her comfort had left with Todd when he departed that morning and there wasn't a supply left to retrieve from. The well was empty.

Then suddenly Brian intervened and whispered, "Mom, it's OK. Why don't you go to your room for a while? I'll handle things here."

Her son had come to her rescue again. He could always read her emotions well enough to anticipate how she felt.

THE NEXT MORNING, FROM THE DIM LIGHT OF HER ROOM, SHE heard only the voices of her son and daughter and the rain beating on the roof.

Though the day of Todd's death betrayed them all with long periods of sunshine, the day of his funeral held a proper tribute with the sorrow of wind and a relentless rain. A rain unlike the northwest norm, not an incessant drizzle but pounding drops.

"You should move home, Izzy. Mom needs you now. I'm sure you can get a job in Seattle," Brian said.

"Brian, mom's capable of having a life here on her own. Let her decide what she wants to do first before you make plans with my life."

"Izzy, you saw her today. She can't stay here alone. Dad would want you to come home and take care of her."

"Mom can take care of herself, Brian. We both know Dad hovered over Mom too much. She might like living alone, you know. Maybe she'll start working again."

"Mom will never need to work again. Dad made sure she's taken care of. She'll want for nothing."

"I'm sure that's true, Brian. But mom likes to paint. It's not like work for her, and she's good at it. She even taught; she loved working with art students. Look, I'll stay for another week, but I have a life of my own in Paris. I have important work. Don't scoff at me."

"You can't possibly care more for your work there. Mom needs you, Izzy."

Vivienne heard the conversation, and she knew she needed to intervene before their words became a battle. Brian only meant well, but Izzy was right. She had a life of her own, and Vivienne didn't want her daughter to give that up for her.

No, I'll be fine, she thought. *I can't let them think I'm this weak. I have to get up.*

When she stepped out of the dark and into the downcast light of her own kitchen, her children were ardently discussing their concerns, with Brian leaning against the kitchen counter and Izzy taking her coveted spot on the barstool at the kitchen counter as she always did as a youth. When she saw them notice her, they immediately ceased to speak, grim lines upon their faces.

I have to stop this.

"Mom," Brian said, "Do you want some coffee?"

"She drinks *tea*, Brian," Isabel said, shocked that her brother didn't even know that much about their mother.

"I'll get you some tea, Mom." Isabel said as she slid from the barstool and took over the sentinel spot from Brian in the kitchen, shooing him from her domain.

Vivienne didn't know where to begin. It had only been a day now that Todd was lying below the cold earth.

Mom...

Just over a week ago, she'd trimmed Todd's dark-brown hair in the bathroom, the dark snips cascaded down to the white tile floor. The snips she took were probably still sitting in the bathroom trash, not knowing their host was now dead.

Vivienne shook her head as if to discard the memory.

"Mom? You OK?" Brian asked.

She hadn't noticed he was standing near her.

She smiled briefly in a way of comfort that meant, *No, I'm not OK. But let's not talk about that.*

He guided her by the arm to the breakfast table nook off the kitchen. "We'll figure this out, Mom."

It's not a puzzle, she wanted to say but glanced into her son's eyes and saw such grief there. "Have you slept, son?"

He was caught off guard by her caring. "I'm...*I'm* fine, Mom."

"How are Katherine and the children?"

"They're all right. We told Sybil."

"They should come over."

"You don't need them running all over right now, Mom."

"Of course, I do. I want them here."

He looked at her, not even considering that she might want her grandchildren around her. "All right. Um, how about I have Katherine bring them over for dinner?"

"That's a great idea. I need to see my granddaughters, and they need to see that I'm all right and that though Grandad is gone, he loved them." Her words choked out at the end even though she hadn't meant for them to. It was a good effort.

At that moment, Isabel brought her tea, and the cup rattled in its saucer as she walked. Though Isabel looked like she had it all together, she didn't, and Vivienne knew her strong daughter needed comfort too. When she sat down, she covered her mother's hand with her own. "Mom, I think we should clean out some of Dad's things from your room while I'm still here. I know it's too soon now, but I can help you."

Vivienne hadn't even considered moving Todd's belongings. Wouldn't she just keep them there, hanging beside her own clothing? "I hadn't thought about removing his things, but I guess you're right. I can't do it today," she said, with a small shake of her head, knowing she was still so far into grief that she couldn't bear making changes or initiating even more of a loss of her husband.

"I know, Mom. Perhaps in a few days. I only wanted you to get used to the idea first."

Brian stirred. "I think I'll go home and clean up. I'll come back later with the girls for dinner." He bent down to kiss his mother.

She hugged him and then said, "Brian, before you go, I want to make something clear to the two of you." She stared at both of them for a moment. "I can take care of myself. It won't be easy, because I loved your father so much and I'll miss him terribly, but I don't want you two to change your lives for me. I'll figure things out on my own. OK?" She looked between the two of them for an agreement.

"That's just it, Mom. You don't have to do it alone. We're here for you. That's what Dad would have wanted," Brian said.

Just as Isabel was about to put forth her argument, Vivienne said, "It's what I want now, Brian. Your father was wonderful to me. Now I have to go on with the rest of my life without him. I can't do that the same way I did before with him. It's just me now. I'll survive. I'll miss him terribly, but I'll survive."

Tears streamed down all their faces with shared grief. "And so will you two." She held them each close to her soul, and then Brian pulled away, wiping his tears as he went toward the front door. They heard him open it and then heard him yell, "Hey, wait!"

Vivienne looked startled at Isabel. "What's going on?"

"I don't know," Isabel said, and ran to the hall leading to the front door where Brian met her.

"What happened?" Isabel asked.

"I don't know. There was some weird guy watching the house out front on the trail behind the trees. I saw him out of the corner of my eye, but when I looked right at him, he took off."

"Did you recognize him?" Vivienne asked.

"No, I didn't even really get a good look at him."

"Maybe it was just a neighbor or someone who wanted to give condolences but just felt weird about it," said Isabel.

"Yeah, maybe," Brian said. "OK, this time, please lock the door and set the alarm behind me, Isabel."

"I'm sure it was nothing, Brian. People are weird about death."

"Yeah, well, please do it anyway," Brian said, and Isabel followed him to the door.

When she returned, she said, "He's just like Dad now."

Vivienne didn't like the sound of that comparison.

"I'll make you breakfast, Mom. A crepe? I finally figured it out. Dad...would be pleased." She muttered the end quietly.

Vivienne smiled, remembering how Todd chided their daughter on her lack of culinary skills even though she lived in France. "He *would* be pleased." She smiled a little, knowing it was so. And then her daughter looked at her from across the kitchen, and they both realized it was her first smile since Todd had left them. *There will be better days to come, won't there?* That was what the smile seemed to say.

Vivienne nodded to her daughter as she began to make a breakfast her father would have enjoyed.

7

Present Day
Lake Union, Washington

LATER THAT SAME EVENING, VIVIENNE AND ISABEL WERE
assembling dinner in the kitchen and waiting for Brian, his wife,
Katherine, and their two daughters, Sybil and Claire to arrive.
They'd opted to leave the girls with a relative for the funeral
proceedings since the oldest child was only four years of age and
the other an infant of six months.

"Why don't we pull Sybil's booster chair out from the closet
for her to sit with us at the big table instead of at the breakfast
nook?"

"I haven't seen my nieces since last Christmas," she said.

Vivienne expected that she was excited, though certainly not
under these circumstances.

"Me too, but, Isabel, let's try to have a happy time and make it
a good experience with the girls here. I don't want you and Brian

arguing, especially over me. It's important to show Sybil we're resilient."

Isabel folded and refolded the dishtowel she was holding without making eye contact with her mother. "Mom, we're not arguing. We just think about these things differently. I know Brian loves you and wants to protect you the way Dad did. He wants me to move back home and in with you." Tears overflowed from her eyes. She wiped them away. "I love you, Mom—please don't think I don't—but I love my life in Paris. I love my work. I...don't want to move back here and give up everything I've accomplished there. I know that makes me selfish."

Vivienne was pulling out a few mystery dishes from the refrigerator from the day before, wondering what they could be and if they were suitable for dinner. She placed a large casserole dish on the counter. "Come here," she said, and held her daughter.

"I miss Daddy so much. I'm so sorry I argued with him, and now...I can't tell him how sorry I am."

Vivienne knew at some point Isabel's contentious relationship with her father would come to the surface. She probably tortured herself when she was alone with her thoughts. "Isabel, your father loved you. You were a challenge to him, no doubt, but he loved you as much as your brother. And look, Brian is wrong to make you feel this way. You shouldn't be guilted like this. I don't want you to leave your life in Paris or give up your career for me. No... I'd never ask that of you. I'm so very proud of you and so was your dad."

Isabel pulled away from the embrace. "Daddy hated that I lived abroad and never became the lawyer he wanted me to be; at least Brian fulfilled his dream."

"Isabel, you father would have loved to have had you live in town and under his sight at all times. We both know that. That doesn't make him less proud of who you became anyway. It's like having a butterfly. The only way you can watch it grow is to let it fly. If you hold it too tight, you'll damage the wings. He wanted to hold you tightly, but he knew he had to let you go; that's painful for a parent. And of course, you didn't give him much choice." She smiled at her daughter and wiped a stray lock of long dark hair out of her face.

"Thank you, Mom."

"Uh, I can hear them coming up the driveway. Go get the booster chair for the table."

As Vivienne popped the mystery casserole into the oven, she heard the front door open. "Vivienne?" Katherine called out.

"I'm in here, my dear," she called from the kitchen.

Katherine came in, carrying six-month-old baby Claire. Vivienne reached around and kissed Katherine on the cheek.

"How are you doing?" Katherine asked her mother-in-law, her face etched with concern.

"I'm OK. Day by day," Vivienne said and smiled. She cooed at baby Claire, who looked just like her aunt, Isabel at that age. Her heart broke all over again knowing that baby Claire wouldn't remember her grandfather at all with losing him at such a young age. *What a shame. Hopefully Sybil will have a few good memories to share.*

"I want you to know...how sorry I am," Katherine began.

"We all are, dear." She couldn't say more because looking into Katherine's blue, crying eyes made her want to weep again too. She loved her daughter-in-law. Brian had chosen well, and she couldn't think of a better match for her son. She was a wonderful wife and a caring mother.

"Sybil is still a little confused. I thought I should warn you. She doesn't quite understand that Grandad's gone. So she might mention him and ask questions. I don't want that to hurt you."

"It's understandable. She's only four. It will take time for her to realize that he's passed away. Seems the terms we use for death are always vague in definition. We'll keep reminding her of the happy times we've had if she gets sad. Where is she?"

"Brian has her with Aunty Isabel in the living room."

"Oh, OK. Isabel was very excited to get to see her nieces again."

Katherine nodded in a way that made Vivienne think she too felt Isabel needed to move back home to take care of her mother. She could tell just by Katherine's expression that she and Brian had discussed the matter.

"I've not made any plans yet, but one thing I do know is that I don't want my children making plans for me or changing their lives to accommodate mine. I'll adjust, it may take time but I'll get there."

Then the convection oven timer rang, and Vivienne moved to take the mystery casserole out while Katherine left to put Claire in her highchair.

"Mom, let me take care of that," Isabel said.

"I don't even know what this casserole is. There was a sticky note that fell off of one of them. It's probably tuna or chicken."

"Don't worry; we have several salads at the table and two hot dishes as well. I don't think we can eat all this food before it goes bad."

"Well, let's try at least. It was very generous of everyone," Vivienne said, and then went into the dining room and hugged her precocious granddaughter, Sybil. While everyone was setting the table set, Vivienne held her granddaughter, whose eyes were very much as brown as her granddad's.

"Grandma, Mommy said you'd need lots of love now 'cause you're very sad," Sybil said, holding her doll between her hands, wringing the doll's cloth arm with her own tiny fists. She rubbed away a tear springing from her wide eyes.

Vivienne couldn't keep her own tears in check then. "Yes. Yes...I'm going to be fine, love. No need for that. I'm going to be just fine. Don't worry about Grandma." She reassured her granddaughter, who'd just turned four. They'd even had a party for her on Lake Union right out the backside of the house on one of the last warm, sunny days of the season. "Your grandad loved us all, and we loved him. We'll miss him very much, but we will live life as before, and we'll keep all our memories of Grandad, the very best ones, for when we're missing him. OK?"

She could see behind those eyes that Sybil was searching for the very best memory she could remember of her grandad. Then she popped the memory out. "Like when he let me ride the Sea-Doo and said, 'All aboard!' really loud?"

"Yes!" She remembered seeing that exact moment too and how Todd had used his entire lung capacity to create the grand gesture. Sybil had stood in her sapphire swimsuit and yellow water-safety vest, dripping wide drops of water on the dock that the sun evaporated at a slow but traceable pace. Her smile had brightened into a wide grin, and she brought her small hands to her mouth, covering her chuckle. Todd loved to amuse Sybil. He'd gently lifted her wet body with her dripping pigtails and sat her in front of him securely while he slowly took her on a little ride through the water.

Memories were gifts now. Vivienne had just learned that from her granddaughter. Like gems, she'd tuck them away to pull out when she missed Todd in the days to come.

"Why don't you help me bring this basket of rolls to the table, and we'll sit down to dinner together."

Sybil nodded in lieu of a reply and reached for the rolls that Vivienne proffered her.

They all sat down at the table, this new family, minus one, for the first time. Todd's chair remained empty next to hers. *That's the way it will be from now on,* she thought. As dishes were passed, she caressed the side arm of Todd's chair, saying to the heavens in a silent voice, *Oh, how you'll be missed.* Then, looking around the table as Isabel and Katherine and her son passed the dishes and filled the plates, she found herself resenting them in a way. How could they participate in normal deeds? Each bite was dust in her mouth, barely passing her throat. She would no longer eat if only she thought the children wouldn't notice. Vivienne barely breathed, each painful breath prolonging her life without her husband, made her ache in ingratitude. Though they said he felt no pain upon his death, Vivienne did not believe this.

"Mother!"

Vivienne looked up, startled with the call of her name.

"You dropped your fork. Are you all right, Mom?" Izzy asked, concerned.

She hadn't noticed. Then she looked down, and there it was, lying where it should not be, beside her foot. She began to reach down to reclaim the lost utensil when her son beat her to it.

"I got it, Mom. Do you need to go lay down?" he whispered to her, when their heads were near, as if they were collaborating on a plan. This question confused her. She'd started to notice a pattern. It seemed their remedy for her grief was to have her lie down all the time. "No, I'm fine." She smiled and then got up to retrieve a clean fork before he could react.

They continued the meal, though she barely knew what she was eating, and when she tasted something spicy, she began picking at the casserole with her fork and then finally laid the fork down and pushed her plate away.

8

P resent
   Lake Union, Washington

THE NEXT WEEK, VIVIENNE WOKE IN HER OVERCAST ROOM, AND
it was the first morning she'd opened her eyes *knowing* what had
taken place days before. The dread washed over her body from
head to foot. She knew immediately why the world was different
instead of coming to the realization all over again, piece by piece
—the accident, the vibrating phone against the palm of her hand,
Brian's reconciled voice of despair.

"So this is how it works. A little less of him day by day."
*Mourning? My heart has utterly broken; only shards remain. I don't want
to hurt any less each day, which only means he's farther and farther away
from me. No, let it hurt as it did the moment I knew he was gone from me
forever. Crush me with the same weight as before; never lighten the blow,
not even for a moment.*

"Mom?"

The door opened and a sliver of artificial light beaconed from the hallway.

"Do you want tea?"

Vivienne blinked, her eyes not yet adjusted to the light, nor did she think they would ever be ready for the full extent of intensity of any given day. She glanced at the clock on the end table of Todd's side of the bed. It read nine o'clock already. "Oh my, I can't believe it's that late."

"Don't worry. You don't have to be anywhere. You can rest. I'll bring you some tea so you wake up slowly. I have a dental appointment later today, but I thought we could work on clearing some of Daddy's things from your closet this morning."

Vivienne wanted to say, No, I don't want to move anything, not the clippings of his hair from the bathroom wastebasket, and I don't want to change the sheets or do anything that will take away his smell from my life. But she didn't. Instead, she said, "Thank you, dear."

Vivienne pulled herself out of the darkness, stretching her cold feet automatically over to Todd's side where the warmth used to linger beneath the covers after he awoke and started his shower. She would always steal the remainder of the cozy heat she found there to drive away the frigid feeling from her toes numb with cold.

The sound of china chattering was distant but gaining in strength, so Vivienne sat up and slipped herself back against her pillows. Isabel entered the room, bearing a cup of steam atop a plate, and when she sat it down, there was also an enticing chocolate chip cookie. "Oh, thank you, Izzy, but I shouldn't have sweets."

"Live a little, Mom," Isabel said, and flashed a brief smile, but it disappeared so quickly Vivienne wasn't sure it was there at all.

"It's OK to say the things you always have, Izzy. You're right. I should live a little."

Isabel gave her a tempered smile after that and sat down at the end of the bed.

Her mother took a sip of her tea while contemplating her daughter. "So you have a dentist appointment?"

Izzy tucked a lock of her dark-brown hair behind her ear. "Yes, I thought while I'm here I should get a cleaning and a checkup."

"Are you seeing Dr. Casey?"

"Yes, of course."

"He's always been the best dentist around."

Vivienne knew there was something else on her daughter's mind and that this was just the way she always meandered around a subject. Vivienne would ask her questions, little questions, unimportant ones, to get her to spill what was really on her mind. But she just didn't have it in her this morning to play the game. "What is it, Isabel? What's bothering you?"

Her daughter was fidgeting with her hands and staring at her own fingers, lost in thought. She shook her head with a sympathetic smile at her mother. "It's nothing; don't worry about it."

"Izzy, just tell me." She felt a little impatient.

Isabel looked at her mother with all seriousness. "I just wanted to tell you about someone I met, but this just isn't the time. I don't want to introduce you to him like this. And..." She choked up. "I wanted him to meet Daddy, and now it's too late."

Vivienne placed her teacup back on its saucer on the night-stand and reached for her daughter. "I'm so sorry, Isabel."

"We've been dating for over a year. He wants to marry me, Mom, and now Daddy won't be able to give me away. I waited too long to tell you both."

Vivienne rocked back and forth, holding her daughter close and stroking her hair as it slickened with her touch.

She whispered to her daughter, "He will give you away as you walk down that aisle someday, when you're ready. Isabel, you've always been so independent, why would it be any other way? He'll be with you still."

Isabel sobbed and nodded her head while her mother patted her back as if she were only five and heartbroken. What the *will* is of death on a loved one remains a mystery to man. There are few greater sorrows that cause a stake through the heart of humans.

"Well, Mom, let's not waste time," Isabel finally said when she sat up and wiped the tears from her eyes that seemed never ending. "We have work to do, and I want to make sure you have a space for yourself without always having to deal with Daddy's stuff when I'm gone."

"I don't mind being reminded of your father, Izzy."

"I know that, but it's not good for you, Mom. Please, for my own piece of mind, let's at least clear out the closet today, put his things away. We can give them to charity or something."

"All right," Vivienne said, and she pulled the covers back and moved her feet to the carpeted flooring. When she stood, her silky nightgown cascaded down to her shins. "I need to take a quick shower, and then we'll get to work." She walked into her hall closet and selected a pair of leggings and a cotton tunic to wear since she knew there would be a lot of bending and lifting.

"Mom, that's like giving up."

"What do you mean? The leggings?"

Then, afraid she would offend her mother, Isabel said, "I... never mind. That's probably a good idea for today actually."

"Izzy, today of all days is not a time for fashion consciousness."

"No, you're right, Mom. I wasn't thinking," She waved her mother off to the shower. "I'll get a few boxes from the garage and several sacks from the kitchen too while you're in there."

Vivienne smirked at her daughter and sidled into the bathroom, and when she looked into the mirror, she felt an overaged image was looking back at her from her reflection. "Oh, Vivienne," she said to herself. Her fawn-brown, shoulder-length hair was mussed. She quickly pulled the length up into a loose bun. "You are going to make it through this." With self-talk she was trying to bolster her self-esteem, though the effort was no more than an attempt before she abandoned the image in the mirror and stepped inside the steaming shower. The glass fogged up quickly, and she remembered so many times after the children left home when Todd would join her in the shower and wrap his arms around her, just caressing her in the warm water, only holding her, loving her until the water turned cold.

How often should one visit her husband's grave? she thought. She imagined that the sod they'd placed over the dirt was starting to take root with all the rain they'd had in the past week. His body in the coffin beneath, decaying even now in his best suit. "Stop!" she told herself. "Stop! Stop this." She wept bitterly and tried to stifle her cries with her own hand and with the pelting shower. "Please stop."

She straightened up and finished washing after a time. She took a deep breath and wiped the final moisture from her eyes, dried off, put on moisturizer and dressed, and then brushed out her hair, again returning it to the usual loose bun after she blow-dried.

With one last look in the mirror, she betrayed her emotions and put on a straight face, there was nothing but sorrow there, and she wanted to mask that from Izzy. There was no need to make this harder on her daughter. For her she should be strong. That's what Todd would have done, had the death been hers instead of his.

When she entered her room again, her bed was perfectly made and Isabel had several boxes opened and sat around the room waiting to be filled with Todd's belongings. Of any trait, her daughter certainly obtained the organization gene from her mother.

Except that today she was losing more of Todd, and her heart clenched when she saw how prepared Isabel was for the task.

She must have made an expression that her daughter caught because she said, "Mom, we *need* to do this. I know it's hard, but living day to day will be better this way when I'm gone. I don't want you to have to deal with this alone."

She nodded and swallowed. "I agree. It's just not easy...letting go."

Isabel turned on the closet light and the bedside lamps. "So, let's begin." Suddenly, as they both stood inside of the rectangular closet, her daughter, with a reverent whisper, said, "I still smell him here."

"Yes, me too," she whispered back, with a kind of appreciation that her daughter too could sense her father there as much as she had.

"Let's begin," Isabel said again, with less confidence than before. Vivienne reached out first to brush her hand against the soft black merino wool suit jacket hanging in front of her. She wanted to be the first to begin. She didn't want the impression that her daughter was the one to start, not in her own mind. She might resent her over time for the act, and she didn't want that.

"I remember this one so well," she said, and picked the hanger off the rack. She breathed in his scent deeply before removing the suit jacket from the rack. She folded the garment over her arm, her daughter watching, no doubt afraid she wasn't going to follow through—or worse yet, break down completely.

Vivienne blew out a breath. "This is in wonderful shape; we should donate it."

Isabel, suddenly relieved, said, "Let's put it in the big box on the bed. I'm sure there will be more to donate than to discard."

As hard as the task was, Vivienne placed the article into the box, his scent leaving her, then suddenly his smell was too much. There was too much of him surrounding her. She needed to get through this quickly or she wouldn't survive. She turned away from the bed and entered the closet again. "All of these white shirts can go. We can just keep them on the hangers. I don't need them," she said, and she put her hands on either side of a two-foot expanse of button-up shirts.

She squeezed them together and then lifted them at the same time and bundled them over her arm. She placed them in the box as well and went for another armload while Isabel too grabbed armloads of clothes. "Why did he have so many? Did he wear them all?"

"Yes and no. He didn't like to get rid of anything of value, you know that."

"But did he wear them?"

"No, not really, but anytime I tried to suggest we lighten the load, he refused. Just look at my side." She gestured with her arm. The whole other side of the closet was jam-packed with articles of all kinds of prints and colors, like a carnival carousel turning round and round, the gregarious colors neither blended nor presented any form or function. The rod, so heavy from its load, bowed in the center, and there were several extra supports put into place for that very reason. Her daughter stared but was suddenly quiet and turned away to retrieve more of her father's things.

That's when they heard the front door open. Vivienne looked at Isabel. Isabel yelled, "Brian? Is that you? We're in Mom's room." Then the door closed again.

"That's odd," Vivienne said, and she went to the hall, but Isabel beat her to it. When they went to the front door, Isabel tested the latch and found it unlocked. She opened the door and looked around. "Are there packages out there? Maybe it was the mailman."

"No, no packages," Isabel said.

"There's mud on the floor there." Vivienne pointed out the tile entryway, where a few perfect boot prints indicated that someone had stopped in the entrance and retreated.

"Those could be from the guests that came yesterday."

"They look fresh to me."

"Well, whoever it was, they're gone now. Let's keep going," Isabel said, returning her attention to the task at hand. Vivienne locked the front door and set the alarm before they returned to the bedroom.

"Were going to need more boxes," Isabel said, after several more armloads of shirts, slacks, and jackets. "I don't recall seeing him wearing half of these." She fingered the softness of a sage-green merino wool sweater. "I would have remembered this one." She held up the V-neck sweater for her mother to see.

Vivienne took a step back to get a better look. "He...proposed to me in that sweater."

"Oh, Mother, I'm sorry." Izzy began to put the sweater away and out of sight.

"No, no..." She reached for the sweater. "I want to keep a few things of him. This is one," she said, and Izzy handed her the sweater. Vivienne smiled. "He was so nervous that night. I knew of course that he was going to propose. He took me to the Four Seasons. Back then it was very swanky. He called ahead and had roses set at our table, with candlelight, and the staff gave us space. It was lovely. He'd reached for my hand across the white table-cloth and somehow had slipped the ring into my palm. There was no doubt I would say yes. I never gave the question a second thought. We belonged together."

She hadn't known she was crying again, but they were happy tears. "That is why your father wanted to keep everything. Things reminded him, and me, of certain memories. Like little time capsules. She held the sweater closer to her and smelled him still within the fibers. "I'll keep this one." She folded the sweater and added it to a dresser drawer.

"Mother, why was Daddy so protective of you? It's like he wanted to keep you in a box like one of his belongings."

Vivienne knew this topic would come up at some point. She didn't want to ever disparage her husband's memory. *How best to answer something I'm still unsure of myself?* She went back into the closet and said, "Your father treasured me and his children. He felt family was something you protected and kept safe."

"But Daddy was excessive, Mom."

"He was. We never really talked to you children about his side of the family much. Though I've always suspected his overprotectiveness came from the events surrounding his mother's death. Except he wasn't super protective until a while later, after we were married."

"But wasn't Daddy orphaned in high school? When his parents died?"

"Yes, that's right. His father was not a kind man. He was especially not kind to your grandmother. He hurt her often, and your father would get into the middle of their arguments, often at his own expense. He tried to protect her from him, but he wasn't always home. She was a beautiful woman. And your dad loved her very much. One day when your dad was at school, his father overdrank and went into a tirade. He beat her until she was unconscious. He panicked then and put her in the truck to rush her to the hospital. It was raining that day, of course. He ran off the bridge up near Bremerton in Kitsap County. They both drowned, but her body was so bruised up they knew her injuries were from more than the accident itself. Your father always blamed himself for not being there to protect her."

Isabel's expression was horror-struck. "I'm so sorry, Mom."

"*I* had nothing to do with it. I didn't even know your father then."

"But you've paid for it. You had to deal with his emotions over losing her that way ever since you married him."

"Izzy, he didn't start this until a little after we were married. I'm not sure why he became so overprotective. Besides, I'm a quiet person. I like solitude. I never minded your father's need to hover over. Sure, every now and then I would push back, and then he would give me the space I needed. Everyone is the owner of their own unique quirks. This was your father's, and perhaps if I were a more social person, it would have been a problem for me, but as it was, we fit perfectly together. You, on the other hand, are far too independent for a partner like your father. You're too much like him." She smiled, and Isabel smiled too.

"Let's go ahead and box these up and put them in the car. We can grab a few more containers from the garage on the way back."

Once they returned they tackled the shoes, and though Vivienne imagined them going through each piece, she no longer felt that way. No, instead she only wanted it over and done with. It was too painful, and she had a limited amount of stamina for this kind of thing today. Memories sprang from those clothes too easily; it was overwhelming. Isabel opened a window to let the moist air in, but it did little to dissipate the dusty closet smell.

Once they were done, Isabel vacuumed out the closet while Vivienne removed her husband's ties. "I should see if Brian would like any of these. I'll certainly save the cufflinks for him, though I doubt they wear those much these days."

Isabel stood wrapping the cord around the vacuum cleaner while listening to her mother but looking at her mother's side of the overpacked closet. "Mom, have you ever heard of the concept of the French wardrobe?"

"No, I can't say that I have," Vivienne said as she wound up several silk ties to set aside for her son.

"It's the way most women from France deal with their clothing. They look at their closets much differently than we do. For instance, they have several basic pieces of the finest materials they can afford but with many fewer items that mix and match with everything else." Isabel looked at her mother's things. "So like, one of the most basic items is a nice, white, tailored, button-up blouse." She chose one from the massive rack in front of her that she'd seen her mother wear several times and held the blouse up. "You can wear this with a black skirt, tan skirt, slacks, or jeans and pair it with a denim jacket, a black blazer, cardigans, and even change that look with the many scarves that you have. It's very versatile, and that's what French women look for in a piece of clothing. They don't wear many prints. Instead they look for good quality pieces that will make many different outfits."

"But I like some color and prints. Sounds a little boring. Although with as much clothing as I have, I never have anything to wear."

"That's just it. The French wardrobe concept ensures you always have something to wear. It uncomplicates life. And when you obtain all the basics, you're allowed to purchase five new items per warm and cold season. So, ten new things a year, and these new purchases you really research and seek out the best quality you can afford. Like, I really want a pair of nice quality patent-leather loafers. I've put aside two hundred dollars for them from my budget, and I'm searching for the perfect pair. I want them to last at least five years, so they have to be well made and comfortable. You can always have printed scarves to dress up an outfit, but see? You're reluctant to wear things over and over. Remember that geometric skirt we bought for me when I was here last Christmas and we went shopping the sales racks?"

"Yes, the one we had tailored at the department store?"

"That's the one. I love that skirt, but because of the print I don't wear it that often. It's too recognizable. So it literally waits in my closet for sufficient time to pass by so I can wear it again. People always comment on it. 'You're wearing that skirt again,' my assistant says. But say I wore a black pencil skirt with a different top, jacket, and scarf every day. No one would even notice. Besides, it's not that big of a deal in France to wear the same articles of clothing day in and day out. And the closets are tiny. You'd never stuff all this in there." Isabel motioned to the mass of clothing hanging before her.

Vivienne looked at the wall of hangers too. "Uncomplicated life...that is something I'd like to work on. But I'm not certain if now is the time. It's hard enough getting rid of your father's things."

Isabel hung her mother's white shirt on the empty space that used to be her father's side. "If you ask me, *now* would be the best time to start. You probably have several items from the basic list hanging in here already. You don't need to hang on to everything, Mom. Start a new trend. You can keep your memories in your own mind where they belong. Sure, keep a few special things, like Daddy's sweater, but please get rid of all of the extra stuff. It's dragging you down. Maybe that was something Daddy needed to deal with in his own past, but you don't, Mom. You have a long life to live. Don't let all these time capsules bury you.

"Just like you wanted me to go after my dreams when I was leaving home, I want you to live freely too. I understand now why daddy did some of the things he did. It makes sense. But without him, these are just things, and they serve you no cathartic purpose."

"All right, dear, I'll think about doing that. Is there a list of the basic items needed?"

"Sure, there's several online. I'll send you one. I also know a stylist in Chicago that helps with this sort of thing."

"Oh, I don't want to go to Chicago, Izzy."

"No, you don't have to go there. They send you things. You talk to them about what you want or need, and she sends you items. My friend works for a company called The Wardrobe. You're assigned a personal stylist and you talk directly to her; it's super easy. You don't even have to go into the department store to try things on anymore. They send them to your door, and you try them on at home to decide if what you already own works for that piece. I love the idea." Isabel checked the time on her watch. "Well, I have just enough time to pack up these last boxes and get them into the car before I need to leave for my dentist appointment. I'll drop them off at the charity house afterward. Will you be OK while I'm gone?"

"Yes, of course. I have a few bills to pay and some paperwork to fill out for Brian and the will executor while you're at the dentist."

Isabel kissed her mom on the cheek and grabbed the last box of items for donation and left.

Vivienne wandered around her room while she heard her daughter leave through the garage. The large empty space felt so bare now that Todd's things were gone. She turned off the walk-in-closet light switch, and with only the gray light of the window shining through, the space didn't feel as devoid of her husband's things as she'd suspected. He was still there with her in her heart and soul, but she felt the fresh air coming through the window and the dim light reflecting on the space. Her white blouse swung slightly on the empty side. She stilled the movement and turned to the chaotic side of her closet for a moment. She rifled through some of them before she finally found what she was looking for. A black pencil skirt, slightly creased by the pressure it endured from the mass of clothing crushing in from all sides. She placed the skirt next to the white shirt and then again dove into the mass and pulled out her favorite black slacks, placing them as well on the other side.

These were the items she wore again and again anyway. In fact, as she contemplated the crowded rack, she realized she only wore about 20 percent of the fifteen-foot rack and probably less than that of all the shoes and accessories lying on the floor and stacked above the rack in precarious heaps.

Though she could breathe better with the fresh air pouring through the window screen in the clean space, she missed Todd and could only do so much so soon, so close to his death.

❧ 9 ❧

S eptember 27, 1987
    Lake Union, Washington
    The Mathis Home

TODD PULLED UP TO THE HOUSE AT THE END OF ANOTHER LONG
work week, hoping to relax with his wife and new daughter over
the weekend. He stopped at the mailbox and picked up the
bundle of letters sitting inside. As he brought the letters in, he
dropped them down on the kitchen counter and then hurriedly
went to peek in on Vivienne and Isabel, when his mother-in-law,
Claire, stopped him in the hallway.

"They're resting. Why don't you get cleaned up for dinner?"

He'd always liked his mother-in-law on the occasional visits he
and Vivienne took, but she was frankly getting on his nerves since
she came to help care for the new baby one week ago. "I'm just
going to look in on them, and then I'll wash up." He sidestepped
her before she could say another word. When he glanced back,
she was smiling and shaking her head. At least she took his defi-

ance in good humor, but if she hadn't, he would have done the same thing.

Todd quietly snuck into the room and found Vivienne sleeping in a sitting position with pillows surrounding her. Her hand was clasped onto the edge of the bassinet, which sat next to the bed. Isabel was keeping her up at all hours of the night, and she barely had time to sleep. Now he was feeling very guilty for even trying to come into the bedroom. But he couldn't help himself. He couldn't see Isabel in the bassinet from his angle by the door, so he gingerly paced as quietly as possible to get a peek at his infant daughter. When he did, her wide, dark eyes were looking back at him. She made no sounds. She was looking wide-eyed around the perimeter of her pink-wall existence. Her hair was the same color as his dark-brown mop, though they thought that might change in time. Her nose was Vivienne's, he thanked the gods, and her little mouth was that of a cherub's; there was no other explanation. And her tiny balled fists made him think she was a born fighter. She smelled fresh from heaven, most of the time. He couldn't help himself. He smiled down at his daughter and reached into the bassinet to pick her up, when suddenly Vivienne bolted up.

"Todd!"

In a soothing tone, he said, "It's OK. It's OK. Why don't you try to sleep?"

"Is she crying? I just fed her," she said, completely out of sorts.

"No. She's just awake and looking around. I'll take her for a bit. Why don't you sleep a little while longer? I'll keep her company."

Vivienne mumbled something as she turned over, exhausted from sleep deprivation, and Todd reached down with his large hands and scooped up baby Isabel, holding her to his chest. To him, she felt like a large warm bag of rice. He didn't know how else to describe her. She needed support for every part of her tiny body, a vulnerability he'd never realized before, and that weakness made him constantly aware of how susceptible this child made him. If anyone ever wanted to hurt him, the only thing they'd have to do was go after Vivienne and now Isabel, his own daughter. The thought of someone trying to hurt them made him hold her slightly tighter in his grasp to keep her safe.

Todd tiptoed out of the bedroom and closed the door behind him. He carried Isabel down the hall, making goofy faces at her and talking to her like an imbecile. When he sat down in the living room chair with her on his lap, she squirmed around. Then his mother-in-law came out of the kitchen and into the living room.

"Todd, you don't need to hold her. I'll take her."

He couldn't help the defense mechanism to thwart her efforts to move in and take his daughter away from him. When Claire reached for her, he blocked her arm with his own. "I *want* to hold my daughter, Claire." He hadn't meant to offend her, but she gave him a look that told him he had.

"OK," she said, backing away. "I just thought, while I'm here, I can take her when Vivienne's sleeping so that you can both get some rest."

He tried to repair the situation. "I know, Claire, but Isabel's never going to be seven days old again, and I want to hold her for a little while when I get home. I think about her all day. When she makes a mess, you can have her back, deal?" He ended with a smirky smile.

They both knew he was in possessive mode, but they each were willing to set that aside to clear the atmosphere. Todd was sure he'd hear about the incident from Vivienne later on, but he'd deal with that then. For now, he only wanted a little uninterrupted time with his baby girl. To stare into her wide, wondering eyes looking around the world and to feel the warm weight of her as she moved her tiny body around while providing that protective barrier between the harsh world and his daughter, this new life he helped bring into this undeserving world.

He'd never known what it would be like to bring a child into this world, and it was both amazing and terrifying at the same time. No one told him, warned him, how vulnerable she would make him feel. Of course, he already felt that way about his young wife, Vivienne, but she'd been able to deal with life's challenges just fine without him on her own, before he'd met her. Not Isabel. This new vulnerability angered him in a way. Why didn't anyone ever warn him? He couldn't even sleep through the night without checking on her every few hours to make sure no one had somehow snuck into the house and kidnapped her. It was maddening.

❧ 10 ❧

P resent
Seattle, WA

THE NEXT THING VIVIENNE FOUND HERSELF DOING WAS hastily donning a jacket from the hall closet, slipping on her shoes, and grabbing her purse and keys. She didn't consciously want to admit where she was going, to avoid an argument with herself.

No matter how she tried, when the question seeped into her mind, she found fresh tears running down her cheeks as she drove on the path that would become all too familiar, she suspected, in the years to come. *How often is too often to visit your husband's grave? And does he now know all my secrets? Do the dead know all?*

She passed through the gates of Calvary Cemetery, and for a moment she was afraid she'd forgotten the way. Then she remembered where Brian had led her and the familiar landmarks, and finally she parked her car and walked up the green slope to the standing stone cross by the newly dug grave bearing her husband's name, with a place for her own name to be etched in the stone someday.

She wanted to say so many things to him. She wanted to say she was sorry for not making him wait just a little longer that morning. But she didn't, and the tears ran down in rivers behind her sunglasses. Her heart was broken all over again, the way she needed it to remain. Getting rid of Todd's things was a mistake, and she needed to make amends to him. Worst of all, she thought she'd feel him here, where his remains were buried, but she didn't. The afternoon sun shied behind the clouds as usual. She felt a chill on the breeze. She felt alone. Where ever her husband was for now, he wasn't there with her.

"I miss you so much. I don't know how I'm going to go on without you. Help...me," she cried, hoping maybe he would come to her then if she begged him to.

Despite the damp grass, she sat down and wept. "What am I going to do without you? You must know my secret now. Someone must have told you there, that my father didn't die at home, as I'd claimed, from the cancer that took his life. He died in prison after murdering the monster that raped my mother long ago. He died in prison of cancer. I'm so sorry I never told you. Please don't think bad of me. Of course, I'm glad he killed the man. Someone should have. I'm just sorry he went to prison, and I didn't want you to know that about him. He was a wonderful father."

Some time passed without a sound. No answers came and therefore no comfort. When she stood her leggings were soaked through with moisture from the clipped, clean, damp lawn. Vivienne's hands shook as she placed a kiss on the stone cross. She walked slowly, uncomforted, back to her waiting car. Her heart was broken as it should be, as it was before.

WHEN SHE RETURNED HOME, SHE QUICKLY CHANGED HER

clothes, wiped her face, made a cup of tea, and then began the paperwork the estate attorney asked her to complete. Isabel returned soon after, and Vivienne tried as she might to act as if she hadn't had a small meltdown after her daughter left the house. "How did your appointment go?" she asked Isabel as she kept her focus on the paperwork at hand.

"Oh, fine. Did you go somewhere?"

"Uh, no."

"Oh, I could have sworn your car was parked on the other side of the driveway when I left."

"Um...do you have any cavities?"

Her daughter chuckled. "No, Mom. I've been a good girl. I brush twice a day."

"Oh, well that's a good thing. Cavities are expensive."

"I thought Dr. Casey was going to ask me if I still wore my retainer there for a minute."

"He didn't?"

"Makes me feel so young every time I come back home."

Vivienne yawned to keep her daughter distracted from her appearance.

"Are you tired, Mom? You've been through a lot today. Do you want to take a nap? Or would you like to go out for dinner?"

Vivienne thought about sitting in a restaurant with her daughter. She just didn't think she was up for that kind of thing yet, maybe never in light of her time at the cemetery today.

"I don't think so," she said but failed to keep the melancholy out of her voice.

"Mom, why don't we go on a hike or take a boat ride this evening, the way you used to like to do? I never understood why Daddy would let you do that."

"Do what? Take the boat out?"

"Yeah, he hated it when you were late home from the grocery store, but he never minded you taking the boat out by yourself."

"Well, he knew I loved painting out there when the light was just right. I needed that time. He also always made sure I knew how to handle the boat by myself. And of course, it has a GPS tracking device, and I have my cell phone with me at all times."

"Do you want to go? It might be a bit soothing. I noticed the lake was pretty calm when I came home. We deserve to get outside after what we did today."

"I'm not sure, Izzy. I might lay down for a bit. I don't really feel like painting, and the light isn't right. Maybe tomorrow evening." She stood and kissed her daughter on the cheek. "I hope you don't mind."

"No, Mom. Of course not. Please, go lay down. I've got some reading to do anyway."

Vivienne left her daughter and felt as though she were escaping to her room this time instead of being sent. When she shut her bedroom door, she saw how empty the room was. Todd's things were gone from her sight. She regretted instantly getting rid of the stuffiness he provided for her. *My God, how I miss him.* She laid down on his side of the bed, buried her face into his pillow, and cried with regret until she fell asleep.

🦋 11 🦋

P
resent
Lake Union, Washington

A FEW DAYS LATER, VIVIENNE FOLDED THE LAST FEW PIECES OF clothing from the dryer that her daughter had asked to throw in with her load before she packed. Today was the day. Isabel was heading back to France after burying her father. Isabel leaving wounded her upon an already fresh wound, but she wouldn't let her pain show, especially since her daughter brightened with the knowledge that she would be headed back today.

She'd overheard her conversation with a male voice on the phone, and she seemed to yearn for something back there. Isabel had a life of her own, even a young man it seemed. She needed to hold her strength at least until after Brian picked them up and saw Isabel off to the airport.

Vivienne couldn't believe how much her life had changed over the last two weeks. She knew she wasn't the only one who felt the shift. She could hear her daughter cry at night when she thought her mother was asleep and how it appeared that her son had aged ten years in a week. He'd barely shaved and wore a look of agony she'd do anything to erase.

"Mom, Brian's here," Isabel called from the living room.

"Are you all ready?" he asked.

"Yes, Mom was just taking my things out of the dryer, and that's it. I'm all packed."

"We'll sure miss you, Izzy," Brian said to his sister, and hugged her. "Come back soon."

Vivienne had noticed how the two of them had become closer in the turmoil of their father's death. At least that was something positive. There was a time they couldn't stand the sight of one another.

"Mother, do you need a jacket? It's raining," Brian had asked her before they left.

She didn't want to answer the question. She felt nothing. She was numb to the cold chill now.

"Mom?"

"Yes, I'll grab my jacket," she said, and quickly walked back to her closet. As if she'd forgotten again, Todd's side of the walk-in closet was empty. She felt so guilty. Why had she let Isabel talk her into getting rid of so many of his things? Only the few basic items that she'd left hanging there were on his side. She reached into the mass of clothes on her own side and grabbed a thick coat. Something to give the children the impression she was warm, though she doubted she would ever be warm again. She felt nothing but icy cold through and through, as she imagined Todd felt deep beneath the ground.

As she went back into the foyer, the door was open, and Brian was loading Isabel's suitcases into the trunk of his Fiat.

Isabel held the passenger car door open for her mother, and after Vivienne locked the front door, she walked through the pouring rain and slid into the seat.

The car door slammed shut, and then they were off down the

rocky driveway to the long drive through traffic on their way to SeaTac airport.

"We have a stop to make first," Isabel said from the backseat.

Vivienne looked at Brian, and he said, "We thought we'd stop by to see Dad before Izzy left for France. Is that OK, Mom? Are you up to visiting the grave so soon?"

Vivienne hid behind her sunglasses. She sniffed. "Of course. I'll be visiting your father often. Izzy should say..." She didn't know really what Isabel should say, and instead of finishing the sentence with effort, she let the unsaid words slide down into nothing. She turned to look out her window but felt Brian looking with concern through the rearview mirror at his sister in the backseat.

Once they arrived, Brian parked quickly and ran around to the other side of the car with an umbrella. He opened the door and ushered out his mother and sister and walked with them to Todd's gravesite.

Isabel was already crying silent tears. She held a bouquet of flowers, though Vivienne had no idea where she'd gotten them. *Had they stopped somewhere, and she was losing time?* As if Isabel sensed her mother's confusion about the bouquet, she said, "I called in for these early this morning. Brian picked them up on the way."

Vivienne nodded as if she understood. *Mystery solved, I'm not crazy. They're just planning things without my knowledge now.* Then suddenly, there they stood in front of the gray cross bearing Todd's name. She would never get used to this. *How could he be down there?* She couldn't remember the color of the silky lining of the coffin suddenly. Was it blue? Or ivory? How could she forget something like that?

Her daughter was kneeling down and placing the bouquet of flowers at rest near the stone. There were many bouquets still nearby, fading a little each day. *Who throws them away when they turn brown and die too?*

Brian stood at her side, shading the rain from her as he wiped something away from his eyes. His leg stammered as he stood, keeping a beat all his own. As a boy, she'd often lay a silent hand upon his arm to remind him of the unconscious agitation. She didn't do that now. Let him do what he needs to do. There's no need to stifle what we do to survive something like this.

Isabel said a few words only she could hear and placed a kiss on her father's name etched in the stone. She stood and smiled at her mother before she embraced her and then cried like she was still a little girl with a broken heart.

Then Brian hugged them both and even his chest ebbed and flowed with emotion. "We're going to be OK. We'll get through this," Brian finally said, more to convince himself than the rest of them.

Vivienne was numb. No tears spilled from her eyes. She was simply empty, though she looked at her daughter and son with empathy. She herself did not cry. Not this time. She'd spent most of her tears in private the day before.

A short silent time later, they were standing at the airport. She didn't even remember the rest of the journey there. After Isabel checked in, she held her carryon bag. She appeared to have resigned herself to spending the rest of the day and night on the airplane, which was a necessary frame of mind for such a long trip.

"All set?" Brian asked his sister.

"I think so," Isabel said, with worried concern as she looked into Vivienne's eyes. "Mother, are you going to be OK?"

Now was the time. Vivienne knew. She had to step up here. From somewhere she pulled the strength—or was it a facade she mustered? "Don't worry about me. Please call as soon as you land or at least text me. I want to know that you're safely there."

"Of course, Mom," Isabel said, and embraced her mother. "Call me anytime, Mom. Why don't you consider coming to see me in Paris when you feel up to it? It would be good for you,

Mom. Please think about it. You can stay for a month even. We could take a trip to Italy or go into London and stay a few days. We can check out the museums. Please think about it. I know you're not ready yet, but I miss spending time with you, and you can do these kinds of things now."

Because your father's dead? was what Vivienne thought her daughter meant but did not say. It was harsh but true. And though Vivienne wasn't ready to hear it yet, she knew her daughter only meant well. "You're right. I'm not ready yet. But I will think about it. I can't imagine leaving here now though."

"I know, Mom. It's just a trip. You'll come back. Just think about coming for a few weeks," Isabel said, and then faced her brother.

"Please, take care of Mom." She seemed to beg him.

"You know I will, Izzy. Take care of yourself, and don't be gone too long. Bring that beau you told me about home to see us. I'd like to meet him."

"I will...soon," Isabel said to her brother, and then smoothed his hair out of his eyes like his mother used to do. "You need a shave. I love you. Give Katherine and my nieces a hug. I wish I'd spent more time with them, but next time I want to take them for a day to myself."

"You got it, sis. I love you too."

She was about to step away when Vivienne reached out and pulled her into another embrace. "Isabel...I love you and so did your father. Very much, never forget that."

Her eyes welled with tears. "I know, Mom. I know that now. I'll be home soon. Don't worry about me. I love you so much."

She stepped away into the mass of people trying to make their way past the gauntlet of security personnel and blew them a kiss before she was engulfed in a sea of strangers standing and going through measures to ensure those who boarded had all safe intentions.

The car felt so quiet with just her and Brian. It was as if Izzy's presence always came as a visitor, and now her family really only consisted of Brian and herself now that Todd was gone.

"Can I take you to lunch, Mom? I have some time before I have to be at the office again."

"No, you don't have to, Brian. I know how busy you are, and you've missed a lot of work lately."

"Mom, I want to. I want to spend some time with you. I don't...I *won't* let you be alone. It kills me that you're in pain. You've lost some weight. I'm worried, Mom. You don't talk much..."

She took in a deep breath. She should have known. Her son was always so observant of her. Even as a little boy, she had to watch what she said around him. "Brian, we can go to lunch. I just don't feel like eating much. I miss him. I'm grieving. I'm learning that he's never coming back to me, and I have to figure out a way to deal with that and I...just haven't yet. I don't know how to do just me. I'm working on it. Don't worry. I'll be fine in time. I'm just not there yet. Where would you like to go for lunch? Should we go to a place your dad liked?"

"Sure," Brian said, and switched lanes after turning on his signal. He exited the next ramp and soon she knew where they were headed. It was a French restaurant that had recently opened, and she had yet to dine there. She'd heard all about the culinary best from her husband after he had dined there on several business occasions. It was amazing to her how men often conducted business camouflaged as a dining experience in their careers. As if breaking bread and a sip of wine was all that was needed to forge the agreements among men; little had changed since the caveman days.

Once seated, she agreed that the atmosphere was grand, with dark wood, gleaming china, and white clothed tables. She could see why her husband would like this restaurant.

"Dad loved this place. I'm sorry he never got a chance to take you."

She smiled. There were a lot of things Todd had promised to do, take her to, or show her, but those days were over. He'd often travel or dine and come back home saying, "I have to take you there. You'll love it." But they never did. It wasn't his fault. They just didn't realize his time would be eliminated so quickly. She relished his memories of such places instead, and now those promises would go unfulfilled. She didn't resent him for broken promises. She just wished they'd had the time. She wished he hadn't died so unexpectedly, without those experiences.

"Dad loved the boeuf bourguignon. I think I'll order that. What would you like, Mom?"

"I...I'm not sure yet. Maybe the halibut." Though she knew that whatever she ate, she wouldn't taste a thing.

Brian folded his menu and ordered for them both. She felt awkward alone here with her son. Her daughter was on her way to Paris, and her husband was underneath the cold, hard ground. She would never get used to this new life, this new reality.

Waiters dressed in crisp, tucked white aprons brought them their entrees, and Brian smiled at some memory as he stared at his bowl of the beef stew cooked in red wine.

"How is yours, Mother?"

She poked at the poached flesh and moved the peas around with her fork. "It's delicious," she said, and swallowed another bite of nothingness, only a texture she didn't really feel.

Her son eyed her for a moment. She thought he might say something but then thought better of it. Once they were done, he drove her back home and walked her to the door. "I need to get back now, Mom. I have a new client appointment in an hour. I hope you don't mind. I'll call you later. Will you be OK?"

"Yes, of course, Brian. You go now and do what you need to do. Don't worry about me. I'll wait for Izzy's call and let you know when she arrives tomorrow."

He kissed her at the door, and when he stepped outside, she expected him to walk away, and with one last wave, she'd send him off. That didn't happen, she felt him on the other side of the door. He stood there waiting. Vivienne's eyes went to the deadbolt. She turned the knob and set the alarm, and then Brian stepped off the porch. Not knowing exactly why, Vivienne let out a sad exhale, like she was doomed to repeat the past. *No, I won't let him do this. It's not healthy for either of us. I've got to get myself together. I must, for everyone's sake.*

Brian was only trying to protect her as his father had done. She watched him drive away and then flipped off the foyer light. She stared into the dark for a moment before wandering inside the house toward the dim light at the end of the hall. "I can live alone," she said in an attempt to convince herself of the inevitable.

❦ 12 ❦

P resent
Seattle, Washington

"Hɪ, I ʜᴇᴀʀ ʏᴏᴜ ᴍᴀᴅᴇ ɪᴛ ᴛʜᴇʀᴇ ѕᴀꜰᴇ ᴀɴᴅ ѕᴏᴜɴᴅ. Hᴏᴡ ᴀʀᴇ you doing?" Brian asked his sister, with concern.

"I'm fine," she said, a bit groggy. "Brian, you know we're nine hours ahead of you, right?"

"Oh, Izzy, I'm sorry. I'll call you back later. I wasn't even thinking of the time difference. Gosh, forgive me."

"Oh, no. You've already woken me up, little brother. What's going on? I talked to mom yesterday. She seemed fine. Not great, but fine."

"Yeah, that's why I'm calling. It's been nearly a month since you left. She's OK. She roams around the house. She's lost a lot of weight. Katherine went over with the girls and hung out a few hours. She seems lost, Izzy. We're not sure what to do. Does she talk to you often?"

"Only a few times. I'm sure this will take time, Brian. You

can't go from living like a couple to a single person and be OK overnight. It's got to be a huge adjustment."

"Well, yeah. I get that, but Izzy, she's losing weight. Katherine said she was at least a size smaller, and Mom was thin to begin with."

"Maybe she needs to get out of that house. I hate to think of her wandering around an empty five-bedroom home we grew up in, with nothing but memories to keep her company."

"Dad wouldn't want us to get rid of the house. He'd want us to keep Mom safe there. That's what he'd want us to do, Izzy. Keep Mom safe with everything he's provided for her."

"Brian...this is about what's best for Mom. Not what Dad would *want* for her but what is *best* for her now without him around. I know Dad would want to keep her safe, but what about keeping Mom happy? Making her feel like she has a life now. What about that? Why not show her there's more to life than her past? It's not fair that she lost dad so soon, but she shouldn't have to suffer the rest of her life for his loss. Let her live, Brian."

"How are we supposed to do that, Izzy? To me, Mom is safe where she is. She'll be happy again when she gets over the trauma of losing Dad. She'll come around in time."

With a slightly raised voice, Isabel said, "Brian, why are you calling me if you don't want my opinion? Look, Dad kept her under lock and key, and because of that, she doesn't even know how to function now. It's not right, Brian. She's our mother. We are obligated to do more than keep her safe. She should be not only allowed to be happy but encouraged to do so."

"OK, OK...I didn't mean to call you to argue. I don't want an argument. I'm worried about Mom. Can you call her and try to cheer her up a little? Maybe encourage her to start painting again or take the boat out like she used to?"

Isabel let a stretch of silence extend before she answered. "Yes, I'll call her. I have a few ideas. I'd mentioned them a few weeks ago, but I'll do it again. Brian, I'd like her to come here for a visit."

Without hesitation, Brian said, "No way, Izzy. That's too much for her. I don't think she's ever even flown without Dad."

"Not yet, but when she's ready. There's nothing wrong with Mom coming to visit me, Brian. But I'll wait until she's ready before I mention it again. She needs time to grieve first. And then time to begin to live again."

"OK, but for now let's just make sure she's happy. I hate seeing her this way."

"Me too, Brian. I want so much more for her. She's always been there for us. It's time we took care of her and encouraged her to go after her dreams like she did for us. It's her turn, Brian. By the way, have you heard anything more about the hit-and-run driver? The sooner they get that guy and put him away, the better."

"That's something else I wanted to mention. As far as the investigation goes, no, I don't know anything more. It's like they say they're working on the case, and then nothing happens. I give them a call at least once a week to keep the case fresh in their minds. I think they know I'm not going to go away like most folks. Something's not right here."

"Really? Why do you say that? People are run over every day by hit-and-run drivers. They never find them."

"It bothers me because...Dad told me once that if anything ever happened to him, that I needed to take over protecting Mom. We were out having a few drinks, and he loosened up a little. Not like Dad, I know, but there was something there he wasn't telling me, and now I suspect Mom has some threat looming over her. It was the way he said it, and he was clenching his napkin into a tiny cube."

"What do you mean? Dad said someone was trying to hurt her?"

"I don't know, Izzy. It was just weird, and now Dad is dead, and I keep thinking of that night at Fred's."

"What's Fred's?"

"It's a bar we sometimes went to after work for a drink."

"Dad never went to bars."

"He did, Izzy. I went with him a few times. It was only with colleagues for one drink at a time. Just for maybe twenty minutes. Fred's is a traditional hangout for lawyers. Nothing major. Rarely did I ever see him have more than one drink."

"Jeez, Dad would only let us have sparkling cider on New Year's, and that's when we were drinking age."

Brian laughed. "Yeah, I remember you giving him a hard time about that."

"I guess if I'd become a lawyer, I would have seen this side of him too."

"That's not a good reason to become a lawyer, Izzy. I think you made the right choice."

"Yeah, well, I'm not so sure now, but I do love my job."

"I know you do. I've got to run, Izzy. I'll let you know anything I find out."

"You'd better. I love you too, bro. Take care."

❧ 13 ❧

P resent
    Lake Union, Washington

VIVIENNE SLEPT UNTIL THE SUN PEEKED THROUGH THE LIGHT-
blue velvet curtains of her bedroom window. It was always Todd
who was the early riser, not her. If she had no one to care for,
she'd sleep until noon after staying up to read until three in the
morning. She wasn't exactly a night owl but needed motivation to
sleep at a reasonable hour, and now she didn't even have a routine
to follow. Nor did she have one person to keep track of. So she fell
into her natural state of sleeping and waking, which was barely
sleeping at night and waking midmorning.

She wasn't proud of this routine. The best people in the world
were early risers, or so she'd been told. Todd was certainly one of
them, both early and a 'best people.' She was neither, and so
waking at a lazy hour was an easy transition to what she considered a sloppier way of life. She blamed the artist in her.

When she did finally awaken, she wasn't sure if she should eat breakfast or lunch or just forget sustenance and wait for dinner, which was what she usually did these days. Living alone for the first time made the decision easy. No need to be fancy. A sandwich would do or one of those reheated frozen meals. There was no need to cook anymore. She discovered this when she visited the market the other night around eleven in the evening and had nothing to eat in the house.

She'd wandered through the pasta aisle with a basket slung over her arm. Though she didn't find anything in those stale packages the least bit appealing. She went through the meat market. What does one purchase to cook for herself alone? Certainly not a roast or a whole chicken. It wasn't even worth heating up the stove for just one person. So, she gave up and went to the frozen-food section and picked up several boxes containing what was promised on the front of the package though she knew those deceptive pictures didn't even matter. Who was she kidding? The meal would taste like all the others and nothing like what was showcased on the front, so delicately labeled and vibrantly photographed. What was inside was a lie, which was how she felt. Without Todd, she was nothing, a lie set in a pretty house that once told a story of a happy family but was now just a former shell of what it once was.

She paid through the self-checkout, and once back inside her car, she realized she hadn't even said one word to anyone within the store. She was a ghost herself. No interaction with a living soul as she was surrounded by darkness and strangers walking with purpose—some of them giggling with others, but mostly they were purposeful.

Once home, Vivienne grabbed a steak knife and poked holes in the cellophane of her beige meal, *Pasta al Carbon*, which looked nothing at all like what was on the package. She was certain, if she opened all seven of the meals she purchased in similar boxes and lined them up, they would all look exactly the same despite the fancy names.

She placed the imposter in the microwave, and after pressing a few buttons, she wandered away into the pantry and perused the wine bottles until she found what she was looking for. Without really thinking if she should, she pulled the cork out of the bottle with a corkscrew and pushed away any cautionary advice that her mind might try to shove at her conscious self.

Once she poured a few inches into a stemmed glass, the microwave beeped and she pulled out the tray carefully with two fingers and sat the tray on the granite countertop. Then Vivienne fished out her iPad for some distraction and found a book on her Kindle app that she'd not finished yet. It was a story about a dead husband and a found violin, and she hesitated to delve into a topic of grief, but the tale was more about the instrument and less about the departed husband. So, she forged on while she stuck her fork into the mass of mush in her tray. She wasn't even hungry but knew she was losing weight, and so she ate mechanically, not tasting a thing.

Then, without thought, she tasted the wine, and that she did momentarily savor. Despite the numbness, the wine tasted good, and she let some of it linger on her tongue. She drank the dry liquid down until she found her glass empty, then she began to outsmart her own common sense, she continued to fill her glass long after the tray was empty and thrown away and the fork was plunked into the empty dishwasher. She moved her iPad into the living room and continued to read and sip.

When the words she no longer comprehended began to blur, she exited out of the reading app and noticed, on the main page, that she had an e-mail. When she checked the inbox, she found the message was from Isabel.

"Mom, here is a link to the French wardrobe list I told you about. Why don't you call me when you have time, and we can look over the list together? Love, Izzy."

"Pssh, I can't call her now. Nooo, that's not a good idea," Vivienne said to her slightly inebriated self, the early-evening hour in

Seattle neared midnight in Paris. Though Izzy was certainly awake since she just sent the e-mail, now would be the perfect time to call. Except that she'd been drinking, and Vivienne would never call her daughter in that condition. So she'd opened the link Isabel referred her to, which took her to a Pinterest graphic post explaining what a French wardrobe entailed and how to achieve that less-complicated lifestyle with your wardrobe.

There was a *starter kit* and a *basics kit*. It was essentially a graphic with all the items listed below the title that you needed to have in your closet. She clicked on the link the graphic came from, which led to a chic French fashion blog.

"I don't know if I need *less* complicated," Vivienne said, swinging her wine glass away from her body, causing the liquid to slosh a little. "Oops, I need a refill." She poured more merlot into her glass and sat the iPad down in the process. The moonlight caught her attention through the window at the end of the dock as it reflected off the water.

She took the wine but left the iPad, slipped into her moccasins at the back door, and went outside into the night. It was chilly. She held the wine glass closer to herself as she wandered down the dark path to the dock, and when she stepped onto the wood platform, her gait swayed even more with the wood platform shifting on the water and the wine flowing through her veins.

The chilly wind seeped between the fibers of her clothes, so she held on tighter to herself and sipped the liquid as it warmed her from within. The moonlight draped over the waves in a sharp contrast of light and dark breaking in intervals. The splashing water told her there was more than wind at work—a storm was either coming or going—though the moon shone bright and crisp, and there wasn't even one cloud to obscure its presence.

There was a time in the past when she'd wander outside on a cold crisp night and walk the dock. Todd always came after her with a blanket and a warm embrace. He'd walk her back inside after they enjoyed their time outside, and he'd cuddle with her by the fireplace until she was sleepy enough to drift off. Now she knew he wasn't coming for her. To guide her back inside. He wasn't bringing the throw blanket to warm her shoulders from the chill. He wasn't coming.

She downed the last of the merlot from her cold glass and looked down at the dark dregs in the cup. She meant to throw the remainder into the water when she flung the glass by the stem over the side, but instead it slipped from her hand and hit the edge of the wooden dock, shattering around her ankles. "Oh, no!" She stepped back, and her heel crunched down on a large shard of glass, crunching beneath the rubber sole of her moccasin. She stumbled on the swaying dock, half tempted to kneel and crawl back the way she'd come so she wouldn't fall over the dock's edge. Instead, she turned and staggered back, guarded against a fall.

Then she heard a noise from the side of the house where there was a door to the garage. "Hello?" she yelled. No one answered. She thought perhaps it was a neighbor putting away his wastebins. Her shoes felt impaled by glass as they scratched the hard surface with each step. She'd have to pull out the shards when she got to the back door so that she didn't damage her flooring.

When she finally made the precarious trip off the dock, she only realized she'd been crying because of the cold, swift-freezing tears on her face.

I'm such a mess. How could I let this happen? She was ashamed she'd endangered herself so foolishly. She could have slipped and drowned without her children ever knowing. Chastising herself for her own foolish behavior with the wine, she finally made the walk to the back door; the journey felt a mile long. Once inside, she went to remove her shoe and realized there was blood covering her sole. The glass was embedded through the rubber and into the tender flesh of her heel.

"Darn it!" she said, only just feeling the pain then. Not wanting to get blood all over her flooring, she sat down on the threshold of the backdoor and slipped off the other shoe. She felt glass in that rubber sole, but her right root was clean when she ran her hands over it. She examined the bottom of her left shoe, which didn't give before when she tried to slip it off, and saw the glass shard holding the shoe in place. She'd been walking on it without knowing she was shoving the glass further into her heel. *How could I not feel that? Am I that numb?* Vivienne grabbed hold of the glass, took a deep breath, and yanked the glass out of her skin. The shoe came away, as well as a stream of bright-red blood.

"Ugh!" Now she felt the stinging pain. With nothing to stem the flow of the blood, she took off the cardigan she was wearing and used that to wrap the wound until she could make the trek to her bathroom and retrieve the first-aid kit without spreading blood all over the house.

In her bathroom, she rummaged for the kit under the sink and then unwrapped her blood-soaked cardigan from her foot and held it over the sink. She ran the tap and watched as the blood flowed with the water down the drain. "Great," she said, wishing her inebriated state wasn't so inebriated at the current moment.

Once she thought the wound was clean enough, she dried it off with a clean towel and applied pressure. The cut eventually stopped bleeding so much, and she took out a large bandage and gauze. After applying ointment to the gauze, she applied the bandage like a suture and used just enough pressure from one end to the other end to keep the wound on her heel from gaping open.

"Probably a good thing I'm a little drunk. That looks like it would hurt like hell."

Though the cut looked like it might need a stitch or two, she was in no condition to drive herself to the emergency room and instead decided the injury could wait until the next day. Then she'd reassess. Not committing to going to the hospital or anywhere else. All of those decisions could wait, in her mind.

She wrapped her bandaged foot in another towel to provide

some cushion when she walked and headed to her bedside. As she walked on the other side of her heel, she stopped at her closet and flipped on the light.

She removed her soiled and bloodied clothing and dropped them into the nearby basket and donned a nightgown she kept on the hook behind the door. By that time the wine was in full effect, and she held onto the jamb to steady her gait. The few items now hanging alone on Todd's old side of the closet were still there. She remembered the list from the starter kit and flipped to that page on the iPad.

One button-up shirt, check.

One pair of black trousers, check.

A black turtleneck, nope.

A striped tee, nope. The perfect black dress, nope. "I have dozens of dresses and the black dress I wore to your funeral but not the *perfect* black dress. How can that be?"

Then, she realized what she'd done. She'd spoken to Todd as if he were standing there beside her now. Shaking her head, she looked down and flipped off the light. Instead of openly admitting she was talking to her dead husband, she made herself comfortable in bed. She felt the guilt but took a deep breath and looked at the list for the starter kit again. While making a list of the items she needed, she checked off those she already owned. It was something new to occupy her time; a project to fill the vast void.

The wound in her heel throbbed as she lay there between the tangled sheets. Finally, for the first time since Todd's death, Vivienne fell asleep having a purpose—and one that was solely her own.

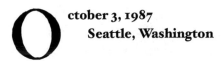

14

O ctober 3, 1987
    Seattle, Washington

WITH MUCH RELUCTANCE, TODD FINALLY SURRENDERED THE
baby to Claire after that new-baby smell transformed into something wholly different. He passed her to her grandmother and
said, "*Now* you can have her."

Claire replied, "Of course. That's the way of men and fathers."

He ignored the sentiment and went to retrieve the mail from
where he'd left it on the table when he'd walked inside earlier.
Among the bills was a plain white envelope, one he presumed was
a letter of congratulations for the birth of his daughter. He
slipped his finger into the side and ripped the seal open. It was
addressed to his name only, and there was no return address.
When he pulled out the contents, there was a sheet of notebook
paper folded around a few photographs. He opened the letter but
held the photos facedown. The letter read: *Dear Mr. Todd Mathis,
Since you've taken my life, I'm taking yours.* Todd's heart began to

hammer in his chest. He reread the letter again, hoping he'd misunderstood the meaning the first time. He'd been warned that there would be days like this when he went to law school.

Days when clients who lost in court would threaten him. Threaten to kill him, his family, and everyone he knew. He remembered the photographs in his sweating palms, and what he saw when he quickly turned them over were two photos of his wife. Candid shots of Vivienne. One, taken as she walked into their local grocery store. The other taken as she was unloading groceries from her car into their home. Both were of her in her late trimester of pregnancy.

Todd slammed the photos on the counter, hitting harder than he intended.

"Is everything OK in there?" called Vivienne's mother.

He was sweating suddenly. "Yeah. I just...everything's OK."

He flipped the letter back over and found there was no salutation at the end. And nothing to indicate where the letter had come from on the return address line. The fact that it had been postmarked in Seattle was no giveaway as to who the culprit might be. Todd immediately shoved the photos and the letter back into the envelope and stuffed them into his briefcase. He didn't want to alert Vivienne or anyone else. The only people he would show them to were the police, and that could wait until tomorrow.

❧ 15 ❧

P resent
Lake Union, Washington

THE NEXT MORNING, VIVIENNE STUMBLED INTO THE LIVING room after hearing her phone chime from somewhere near the foyer. She finally found the cell while doing her best to ignore the persistent thrumming in her head. As she grabbed her phone, the call ended as soon as she looked at the screen. "Perfect," she mumbled, and then she realized her foot was still bandaged in a towel, and it hurt like hell.

Then the night before came back to her in a rush. "Oh my God, I could have killed myself out there. Never again." She rubbed her forehead and looked at the screen of her phone to see whose call she'd missed.

"Izzy," she said. "Oh darn." She quickly looked at the clock and realized it was past ten in the morning and calculated that the time in Paris was seven in the evening. She wanted to call Isabel back right away, but first she needed water and a few painkillers to clear her head and perhaps a cup of coffee or two before she could think clearly. Once she went to the kitchen, she maneuvered carefully, doing her best to walk on the side of her foot. *The injury will have to wait,* she thought to herself.

Vivienne brewed a cup of coffee and knew she'd better eat something to chase the painkiller or, with the present state of her stomach, she might lose everything and feel even worse than she did before. She grabbed a paper cup and scooped about a third of a cup of quick minute-oatmeal from a large cardboard canister in the pantry. Into the cup, she added about a tablespoon of brown sugar. She was never into fast food, but this was as quick as she could make a hearty breakfast. It was something she'd developed and refined over the years without having to measure anything when the kids were little and running late to school. To that, she added a few raisins and walnuts and then poured milk in the cup to about two-thirds full. She popped the cup into the microwave and nuked the simple concoction for two minutes. Her next mission was coffee. Though she usually drank tea, coffee was necessary this morning, the stronger the better. She usually took the brew black, but this morning she couldn't bear the bitter taste. She added a teaspoon of sugar and bloop of half-and-half from the fridge.

While she sipped the necessary caffeine, she began to remember something—her closet. She was going to do it. She'd decided last night. She wanted to do something, something worthwhile, and why not start with her closet? It wasn't like there was anything else going on. Nothing to keep her busy or to keep life the least bit interesting. Then the microwave beeped, and she let the cup of oatmeal set another minute while she drank more of her coffee. When she took the oatmeal cup out, she stirred the contents well. The oatmeal was a bit runny, but she knew from experience that as the mixture sat on the counter, it would thicken perfectly. Her stomach was beginning to ache without proper food, painkillers dissolving in her stomach with the addition of strong coffee. So she stirred the oatmeal a little more and then took a bite, even though it was still a bit too hot. Scalding her mouth was a risk she was willing to take to stop the pain in her stomach from becoming worse and nausea setting in.

Once she was finished and feeling halfway human, she called her daughter back, not wanting to keep her up too late in the evening there in Paris. "Hi, Izzy. You called?"

"Yeah, Mom. Where were you last night? You usually answer pretty quickly. I was getting worried."

"Oh, don't worry, Izzy. I was in the shower. I stayed up a bit late last night reading and slept in this morning," Vivienne said as she looked to her wrapped foot. Bright-red blood was seeping through the towel. She'd have to take care of that next.

"OK. I hope you're sleeping well," Izzy said, still concerned.

"No, don't worry about me. I'm fine. I'm getting through things. It hasn't been easy, but I don't want you to worry about me. I started on pulling things out of my closet last night. I'm going to work on that again today."

"You did! That's great, Mom. That's actually why I'm calling. I got a hold of my friend. Her name is Veronica, and she works for The Wardrobe. She's a stylist. I set you up with her. She's an older lady—well, I mean, she's older than me and younger than you. She'll call you in a few days."

"Oh. Do I really need a stylist? I can do this myself."

"I'm sure you could, Mom. It's more about knowing brands now and what will work for you and what won't. I told her you wouldn't want a fitting or to go into the store, so it's all online. I sent you the link, and she just needs your sizes. You can go through the list and make a new one with things you need. She'll send you those as well as outfits you might not have considered."

"Well...I guess that's all right. I want to pare way down though, so I don't want a bunch of extra stuff that I don't really need, like the stuff I already have in my closet."

"Wow, you really have turned a new leaf. That's no problem. You send the items you don't want back to her in the box that they send you. It's really easy. They even schedule a pickup for you. What are you going to do with all your old clothes?"

"Well, I can give them away or I could sell them online to help pay for the new purchases."

"Yes, that's exactly what my friend did. She had a closet as big as yours and only wore a few items over and over. I wish I was there to help you."

"That's OK. I think this is something I need to do by myself. It's kind of cathartic. It gives me something to do while I'm thinking of how I want to spend my time. I can't just keep roaming around this house alone forever."

"Have you started painting again or teaching?"

"I haven't started a new painting yet. I might take the boat out later today. I haven't decided. I just need something to do for now to keep my mind from roaming, and cleaning out my closet will be a good start. Thank you for introducing me to this. I'm excited to get going on the purge."

"Me too, Mom. Listen, I have a meeting early tomorrow morning, and I need to get to bed early. I hope you don't mind."

"No, Izzy, do what you need to do."

"Mom, I'm serious about you coming over here to visit me. Please think about it."

"I will. I'm not ready yet, dear, but I'm thinking about it. Believe me. I miss you already and I feel so old. I feel like I need to accomplish a few things in my life before it's too late."

"You're not old, Mom. There's a lot of life still ahead. Please keep moving forward. You used to tell me that all the time; I can't believe I just used that on you."

Vivienne chuckled. "It was good advice then. I'm glad you remembered. I will. I'll keep moving forward. Maybe baby steps at first, but I will. I love you, Isabel. Get some sleep."

"I love you too, Mom. Good night."

"Whew," Vivienne said, after hanging up. *I got through that without embarrassing myself.*

After taking a few more bites of her breakfast, Vivienne scanned her e-mail on her iPad and noted a new message from Isabel last night as well as a new one from the stylist from The Wardrobe. "They didn't waste any time, did they?"

She was a little apprehensive about this new stylist thing. But she decided to take new ideas in stride. She was embarking on a new life, and she might as well try new things, even if they made her a little uncomfortable.

"First things first." She held up her foot, which was beginning to pulse even more. She wasn't sure if she'd need stitches or not, and now was the best time to find out. She emptied her coffee cup and scraped the last remnants of oatmeal from her cup. After tossing the paper cup into the recycling and spoon into the empty dishwasher next to the lone fork from night before, she said, "I'm going to have to start handwashing my own dishes. This is such a waste. At this rate it will take me a week to fill it up by myself." It wasn't lost on her that talking to oneself was another sign of being a widow. Suddenly living alone came with a few surprises.

Once she hobbled to the bathroom, she sat on the closed lid of the commode and carefully unwrapped her foot. The towel stuck to the part where the blood had dried and she wet another old towel with the hottest water from the faucet and then held that in place for a while, until she thought the dried blood might peel away better without ripping the wound wide open again. Then she cleaned up the cut. The inch long injury was concerning though more so the depth worried her. But she thought she could keep it bandaged without too much of a problem and decided it didn't warrant a trip all the way to the doctor's office.

As she showered, she tried to avoid opening the wound too much. Blood filtered down the drain. She watched as a red line swirled in the water current like a tiny red river as it mixed into a larger clear ocean. Then she dried off and added more antibiotic ointment and another clean bandage to the cut, hoping perhaps it would heal on its own. She'd keep an eye on it and would try to walk on the outside of her foot for the next few days.

Afterward, she took the time to apply makeup for the first time since Todd's death, and instead of grabbing sweats and one of his shirts to wear throughout the day, as usual, she chose the white button-up shirt and black slacks hanging on the other side of the closet. Then she added styling crème to her long dark-blond hair and took the time to part her hair into sections and blow dry it the way the hairdresser had taught her the last time she was at the beauty salon. Just that much of an effort made her feel ten times better than she had in the past month, even with a slight hangover from the night before. It was the accident on the dock that made her take more effort.

The only problem was that her standard size-eight slacks felt loose and baggy. She knew she wasn't eating normally, but perhaps having lost a little weight wasn't such a bad thing. She decided she would look at her diet and pledged to also start eating healthier—and perhaps a little exercise wouldn't hurt either.

Thinking back on what might have happened out there on the dock last night by herself, she felt ashamed. What if she'd really injured herself, or worse? Her children would never forgive her. "Well, that's the end of that. I have to start taking better care of myself."

Vivienne put on a pair of black flats and a sweater. She grabbed a broom and went out the back door to clean up any remaining glass shards from the dock. Though it was a private dock, she didn't want any evidence of her carelessness last night left behind, and she didn't want to forget to clean it up in case Brian happened by and somehow saw what she had done. The incident would only worry him, and he'd question her sanity. Heck, she questioned her own sanity. No, it was time to get out more and make some changes.

The sun was up, and there wasn't a cloud in the sky. She couldn't help but blink from the sun's bright rays. She felt alive and consciously breathed the fresh damp air in deeply. It was good to be outside again. Vivienne took cautious steps down to the dock, being careful of her heel. She saw the darkened blood drops making a trail down the dock. "Oh, geez, I'll need to clean that up too." But first she took the broom and went for the glass shards left over from the night before, sweeping what she could into the attached dust pan. The rest went overboard, along with her guilt. It was nice to have a glass of wine, but she'd limit her intake to a single glass when she was alone and when she felt like relaxing a bit.

The wind whipped at her long hair, and on her way back to the house, she saw a neighbor out walking his dog. He'd waved to her from the street before, and his golden retriever always seemed like the happiest dog in the world when he was out on a walk with his owner. She'd swear the dog was smiling as his long golden fur fluttered in the wind. "Nice day, isn't it?" the neighbor called to her.

"It certainly is," she replied as they neared her gate. She walked to the side of the house, with the dustpan full of glass to dump in the trash canister. Then she remembered the noise she'd detected last night coming from this side of the house. She checked the lock on the garage door and found it locked, but there were several scratches on the knob itself. It may have been that way for a long time since Todd was the one who usually put out the trash. She rarely used the door.

The neighbor stopped alongside the gate leading to the road as she neared, distracting her from her thoughts. "Did you hurt yourself, Vivienne?" he asked, as he noticed she was hobbling.

Embarrassed, she said, "Oh, no. I dropped a glass last night and cut my foot on a shard. It's nothing really, just a little cut."

He stalled and looked at her with concerned eyes as his glasses slipped down his nose. "Well, be careful, Vivienne. I know how hard it is when you lose your spouse. Are you doing OK? It's a huge adjustment."

She nodded. Her elderly neighbor had lost his wife over ten years earlier; he'd only recently remarried. "It has been an adjustment for sure. I'm getting better. A little more each day." She smiled to reassure him.

He patted her on the shoulder. "They say time heals all wounds. I'm not sure about that. I miss Margaret terribly, even now, but life goes on, and so must we. If you need *anything*, please let me know. We're all here for you, Vivienne." He gave her a consoling and knowing smile.

She smiled back. There was a time she would have thought his words were condescending, but he was right, and she chose to take the sage advice in the spirit it was intended. "Thank you, Meryl. I was just thinking maybe I need to get a dog. I'm talking to myself way too much lately." She laughed and thought maybe she shouldn't be divulging that kind of information to her neighbor.

"They are great companions. The shelters are full of good friends. Maybe wait a month or two, if I were you. You might need a little time to figure things out before you're settled in your new life. Take trips, go back to work, do whatever you want away from home and then decide. They can be a lot of work, but when you know you're settled, get a pet—when you know it's right, when you can see the light at the end of the tunnel."

She agreed. This man was full of good knowledge today. "That's great advice. I should pay you." She chuckled.

"Nope. We're all in this life together. This was advice I received in those dark days following Margaret's death. I'm happy to pass it along."

He waved good-bye to her and continued on his walk. She went back inside the house feeling refreshed after being outside a little and decided the house was too stuffy with stagnant air from days past. She opened a few windows and then decided to get to work, vowing that this day would not be another where she succumbed to grief fading into the next. No, today she would grow and take even another step forward, like she promised Izzy.

First though, she decided to put on a belt because her slacks kept riding down. She'd have to put those on the to-be-replaced list if she was going to maintain this new slimmer size in longevity.

She'd always been on the slim side, but after being a wife and mother, she always taste-tested her recipes before serving them, and that included any cookie dough or cake batter. While a size eight was perfectly fine, she'd wanted to be a size six or dare to even slim down to a four, though the effort never appealed to her. Todd liked her the way she was and even discouraged her from trying to lose weight.

She wrestled a few more boxes and trash bags and maneuvered them into her room before she began purging her closet, and then with her starter-kit list in hand, she began pulling those items she already owned and placed them on the sparse rack with the others.

She already owned a nice pair of Michael Kors black leather pumps, and so she pulled those over to the new side of the closet and marked that item off her list. Then she needed a trench coat. She didn't own one, and why she didn't own one in Seattle made no sense at all with the persistent inclement weather. So that went to the top of her needs list. Then there was a black turtle-neck. She owned a T-shirt style but not a fine-knit sweater version. The T-shirt version fit her nicely, and she didn't see a reason to replace it, at least not yet. So she kept that one and added it to the new rack. "A striped Breton shirt? Nope. Perfect white tee, nope. Dark skinny jeans, nope. The perfect black dress, nope. Black trousers, uh"—she looked down—"nope. A black blazer, nope. Black loafers, nope, but I have nice black flats so I'll use those instead of the loafers." She made the adjustment on her list. "Leopard flats? I've never owned anything leopard before in my life. Hmm," she thought. She wasn't opposed to the idea; she always thought a leopard print might be too garish, but she was willing to give the print a try in small doses.

While she pushed the boundaries of her comfort zone, she took a look at the next step, the basics list, and quickly pulled the items she already owned. "Wool winter coat, black pencil skirt, check. Black cardigan, check. Black boots, check. Black purse, check. Pearl earrings, check; pearl necklace, check; and nude nylons, check. I've got those items, but the rest will go on the needs list."

Then she had a thought. "Gosh, this could get expensive." She felt the silky sleeve of a red dress she wore once to an event with her husband three years ago and never wore again. "I'll sell these to pay for the new pieces."

Vivienne began to pick up armloads of clothes and rehung the items she no longer needed in Isabel's empty closet. She continued to make small trips until everything was purged except for the few items remaining that she needed. She rearranged the items into sections from blouses to longer items and then from light to dark hues. Afterward she felt relieved, better, and refreshed. Only twenty items remained, and for some reason she didn't feel at a loss. Instead she felt reinvigorated. These were her most-worn items anyway. She wished she'd embarked on this venture long ago. This knowledge would have saved her countless hours over time standing before a mass of clothing so diverse she could never decide what to wear. What a frustration knowing how blind you've been.

By then, her stomach began to grumble. It was lunchtime, and she wandered into the kitchen for water and whatever she could scrounge up out of the refrigerator. When she opened the door, she was met with only wilted lettuce, dried floppy carrots, a carton of spoiled milk and nothing that looked remotely edible. So she pulled the trashcan over to the refrigerator and began tossing everything within a reasonable expiration date. By the time she was done, the whole trashcan was filled to the brim. She pulled out the trash bag and brought the contents to the outside bin. When she returned she cleaned the inside of the refrigerator from top to bottom as well as the freezer section. *This too must be redone.*

Then she went through the pantry and tossed anything with an expiration date as well as anything she knew she would not eat on her own. The latter items she set into a box and would drop them off at the food-donation bin in the entrance of her local grocery store. Pretty soon, the pantry shelves were empty too, except for a few staples. *Now is the time to start eating better*, she thought and set out to find a meal app with a healthy option for single servings on her iPad.

She loved to cook but hated to waste food, and she wasn't one for leftovers day after day, so when she found an option that was perfect for her, she downloaded the app. It contained a good balance of fresh produce and select meats so that she could either cook all her meals for the week at once, or she could prepare them day by day. The grocery list was already provided for her, and she set to work. Not only did she have a lot of items to drop off at the local charity, but she also had a list of groceries to pick up. It was already late afternoon, so she grabbed her keys and headed out after loading all the donations into her car.

The drive didn't take long for her to drop off the items for charity at the donation center. She simply drove up, and two men came out of the store to retrieve her items and handed her a tax receipt. The stop took less than a minute, and she was happy that those things would now go toward something good.

She waved good-bye and then headed to the grocery store after that and again dropped off the food donations into the bin on her way into the market.

With her iPad in hand and the meal plan app open, Vivienne went from aisle to aisle selecting the ingredients she needed to keep herself healthy. Shopping for one individual was very different, but she vowed to take better care of herself, and those frozen meals just didn't sound appealing anymore. She'd always had someone else to cook and care for. However, after the last few days, she saw that she needed to shift that nurturing spirit to the keeping of herself, and that was an adjustment for her but one she was willing to make.

As she stood in the checkout line after picking the ripest vegetables by hand and selecting the best cuts of meats, Brian texted her and asked if she was doing OK. She reassured him that she was fine and that at the moment she was at the grocery store. She thought that was enough to reassure her son that she was in good health.

On her way home, the sun was just beginning to wane, with light ribbons of ruby on the horizon. The sight was lovely. "Great evening to take the boat out." She reminded herself that today was the first day since Todd's death that she felt alive and that, with a little more effort, she could begin to live again.

❧ 16 ❧

P resent
  Lake Union, Washington

AFTER HASTILY PUTTING AWAY HER GROCERIES, VIVIENNE checked the time and couldn't wait another second. She'd decided on her drive home that she would take the boat out if she returned in time. She and Todd had made their trek through the Ballard Locks almost every evening so that she could paint the sunsets and he could relax after a long day at work. There was something about the soothing rocking of the boat that relaxed him in the evenings. He often said having her out on the water to himself made him feel secure. She'd always thought that was odd. They'd often return late in the evening and simply slip into bed after returning without flipping on a single light.

And now, this routine was something she needed even without Todd by her side. She grabbed her art bag with her canvas and materials after she changed. On her way out the back door to the dock, she locked the door and put her cell phone into her bag as well. She always kept her art bag so that she was ready to go when Todd came home and needed to take the boat out. She'd also taken the boat out to Puget Sound many times on her own. Todd never seemed to mind her boating trips, only her car trips. She never understood why.

To get to Puget Sound, she first had to navigate through the Ballard Locks. Once you'd been through there a time or two, the routine wasn't difficult. The workers even began to recognize you and waved on occasion. Much like getting in line for a ferry, she pulled her boat up near the one on the right side. A state police boat was already on the left. The officer waved to her, and she waved back once she was fastened in the queue. Then the water began to rise and the boats along with it. Once they were at the right level, the gates opened and one by one as they filtered in line, they repeated that process to exit.

On the way she passed the many boathouses, along with the one used in the famous movie with Tom Hanks. The waves were nearly placid, which was unusual for that time of day in the fall, making reflections hard to resist for a painter.

The sun was beginning to set, and she loved how the evergreens and buildings lining the sound started to look like black shadows against the pastel sky. Like before, a crimson line began to accentuate the sky below a pale blue and above the golden light of the receding sun. In another second, the light would be at the perfect point to capture the scene, and she quickly settled on a tranquil spot in the sound and pulled out her painting equipment. She worked quickly. Other boats passed her by, occasionally sending a wave that she rode out, but pretty soon the chill became too much to bear. She usually brought a thermos of hot Earl Grey tea to enjoy when it was too dark to paint, but the light of the sunset was too enticing to leave. The sunset was something she and Todd enjoyed, and he would often wrap his arms around her while they watched it dwindle into the sea. They'd then make their way back through the locks at night and back into Lake Union.

Now, she was alone. Todd forever gone from her life, yet he still surrounded her even in death. Here, in the late evening watching the sunset, he was with her still. She felt him there alongside her as the last golden light ceased to be.

On her way back, she wasn't sad. She'd enjoyed her time, and when she pulled up to the dock and secured the boat for the evening, she walked back inside. No one was in sight along the shore this time of night, as if it all belonged to her alone.

Once inside she realized she'd forgotten to check the mail, and she walked out the front door in total pitch dark. The sun was long gone, but it was still early evening. The gravel driveway crunched under her feet, and when she unlocked the mailbox door, she grabbed the large bundle of mail from within the dark cavern.

Back in the house, she tossed the flyers and magazines into the recycle bin. She didn't care to look at them. Then she glanced at the letters. Most every envelope was addressed to Todd, except for a few that were addressed to her, and those she knew were condolence cards. It was so odd seeing her name written alone, by itself, in singular. Once she took the time to inform the various entities of her husband's death, she realized the envelopes would begin to be addressed to her instead, and Todd's name would soon fade away. She wasn't sure how she felt about that. Parts of her wanted to see his name everywhere she turned, but then another part of her wanted, needed, her own identity now that he was gone. The reminders of Todd were endless, and now she was beginning to see that she needed to find her own way if she were to survive this loss of him.

So she wrote down all the business mail or bill invoices and created a list of companies to notify. List making was something she liked to do to keep her on track. Once she completed the task, she left the list on the kitchen desk counter to tackle in the morning. For now, she intended to make herself dinner, so she began chopping vegetables and marinating thinly sliced sirloin for a quick stir-fry with an easy-to-make, single-serving size of precooked brown rice. Once dinner was complete, she served herself like she would have her family in years past. She poured herself a full glass of water and squeezed one whole lemon into the water to drink with her dinner. She usually did this before she went to bed, but she was eating a late dinner tonight, and it seemed the right thing to do.

While she ate, she listened to relaxing music from her iPad app and flipped through a department store app. She found several items that might work for her new wardrobe and added them to her wish list. She'd plan to share those items with her stylist as examples of things she liked when she spoke with her.

Then the light of the moon reflecting off of the water caught her eye outside on the lake. She and Todd used to sit and drink a bottle of chardonnay while watching the spectacular views in the early fall from their own back deck. Those were memories she would cherish for a lifetime. Soon she found herself sitting with a cold plate. She took a deep breath and steeled herself away from the lingering depression threatening to consume her.

It had been her first good day since his death. Part of her wanted to have a complete and total breakdown, let grief overtake her again. But the other part told her not to dare. She'd put too much effort into having a good day to ruin it now. She stood and picked up her plate and brought it to the kitchen sink and turned on the little overhead light. Then she washed her plate and the skillet she used, along with the utensils, and set them out to dry. No need to run the dishwasher yet. When she was done, she stared out at the lake one last time as the silver light of the moon played on the waves and then went to her bedroom.

She changed, washed her face, moisturized, and checked the wound on her foot. There was a red circle developing around the circumference of the now-tender cut. She wasn't sure if it was healing right but changed the dressing and thought she'd check it out again tomorrow morning. She slipped between her sheets with her night light on and read from her Kindle app until she let sleep overtake her. This was a good day, and she wasn't going to let her hard-won efforts go away now. Not when she was this close to the end.

❧ 17 ❧

O ctober 5, 1987
   Seattle, Washington
   Fred's Bar

TODD PUSHED OPEN THE FAMILIAR DARK WOOD SWINGING
door. Walking into Fred's was like walking into the nineteenth
century. Everything was made of either dark ornately carved
mahogany wood, gleaming brass, or crushed red velvet. The
aroma even had a distinctly historic smell of a time when most
men smoked cigars, which always reminded Todd of a creamy
floral. It was a characteristic trait of times past. Unlike the new
bars of Seattle, with their industrial garage feel, this place never
seemed to comply with modern times, and most locals wouldn't
have had it any other way. Fred's was a landmark of Seattle, a place
where time didn't affect the patrons. It was simply a favored spot
for those who had something on their minds and brothers that
needed an ear to help make sense of it all.

Todd sat at the bar on a heavy wooden stool with Charlie after
work at the end of another long week. They'd both pulled their

collars loose somewhere on the walk between leaving the office and arriving at the tavern.

He had a Tom Collins sitting in front of him and stirred the chamois liquid among the little ice cubes, chasing the red cherry with a tiny straw. He picked up the little diminutive straw and wondered why it was even in the shape of a straw? It was too small to drink from. Why wasn't it just a solid stick? He'd never understand why some things just *were* in life. No real explanation as to why something *was*.

Charlie was nursing a Grey Goose martini, sipping it slowly and shuttering with each attempt.

"What do you mean there's nothing they can do? Whoever this is directly threatened my wife."

"Todd, as a lawyer, you are going to have death threats against you, your children, your wife, your parents, and your dog. Hell, even your great-grandchildren and your mailman."

Todd thought about that. "He can kill the mailman. Just stay away from my family."

"Geez, what's wrong with your mailman?"

"Oh, nothing. He's Russian. Guess that's not reason enough to kill him though."

Charlie laughed and shook his head. "No man, that's not good enough reason to offer him up instead. Look, don't worry about this. He's just some loon; he'll move on soon. Loons have short attention spans. And in prison they tend to have short lifespans as well."

"What makes you think he's in prison?"

"I don't know. It's a generic envelope. Anyone could have taken the photos; his wife, a cousin, a gang member even. But mostly because of the threat itself. He could have just had someone else write up the letter, grab her photographs, and mailed the letter all on his instruction. He may never have even seen the letter itself."

Todd leaned his elbows on the bar, defeated. He hung his

head. "He took my wife's pictures when she was vulnerable and pregnant. He followed her to the grocery store, man."

"Hey, if it were my wife, I'd be just as pissed off. But truthfully, he's not going to do anything. He either just wants the attention or he's trying to rattle you. Do you have any idea who it could be? Past client?"

He shook his head, "I've been racking my brain. I don't really know. It could be one of twenty different guys."

"What did the cops say?"

"Same thing you said. Just a threat. Don't worry about it."

"But they're taking the case seriously, right?"

"Yeah, they kept the letter and stuff. Said they'd follow up on any leads I give them, but there wasn't much to go on. God, Charlie, it makes me sick to my stomach to think this nut might touch my family."

Charlie clapped him on the shoulder. "Todd, I understand how you feel. If it makes you feel any better, have her learn about firearm safety. Teach her how to defend herself. Get her a concealed-carry license even."

"I haven't told her about any of this."

"What? You didn't tell her about the letter?"

"No. We have a new baby. I don't want to freak her out right now. She barely gets to sleep. Would you?"

Charlie thought about it for a bit. "No, you're probably right. It would only make her worry, and trust me; new mothers do not like to feel threatened. She doesn't need that right now for sure. And the letter directly threatened her."

"I'm pretty sure that was the intent."

"Yeah, but you can't live your life this way, or they win. You see? For all we know the author is another crazy lawyer or the culprit could even be one of those damn judges. Ellington has it out for you, now that I'm thinking about it," Charlie said, contemplating different scenarios.

Todd laughed, remembering how the old judge gave him the

evil eye recently when he corrected him on a previous court order he'd forgotten, "It wasn't Ellington. That guy needs to go though; he's losing his memory. Look, I need to run, but thanks," Todd said as he slapped a few dollars on the bar, waved to the bartender, and then slid off his stool. "And Charlie, please keep this to yourself. I don't want anyone else to know about these threats."

"No problem, buddy."

18

P resent
  Lake Union, Washington

WAKING FINALLY AT A NORMAL HOUR OF THE MORNING,
Vivienne felt refreshed and eager to get to her list, which was to
respond to her newly appointed stylist. So after breakfast, she did
a load of laundry, finding one of Todd's shirts in the dryer. She
wasn't sure how she missed it before, but she didn't let it break
her. "Nope, not today," she said, determined to hold on to her new
life alone.

After taking out the trash, she took the list of entities she
needed to notify from her kitchen desk, promising to herself to
notify at least the first five companies that her husband was
deceased and to move all information into her own name.

Accomplishing a chunk of this every day would be just enough
to still let her remain sane. Any more and she'd dissolve into a
crying mess again, and that was something she wanted to avoid.
Each weekday, she checked the mail and listed at the bottom all

the addresses of all the recipients she needed to contact, and each morning she'd tackled the top five, slashing a pencil line through the ones completed.

After she made those calls, she admittedly felt a bit drained and had a brief thought of only managing three for each day. She made a deal with herself to try five and see how that went. The hardest part was hearing the words "Sorry for your loss, Mrs. Mathis," which was repeated over and over again. She was starting to resent the term itself. *I didn't lose him. He was killed. He died. He's not lost somewhere.*

She longed for the day when she didn't have to hear that phrase. To reward herself, she then called her new stylist. When the stylist answered, she was a bit nervous. Vivienne thought she'd set up a time for this, but instead the stylist answered her own number.

"Hello, Mrs. Mathis, I've been expecting your call. I met your daughter at the University of Washington a few years ago. We've kept in touch ever since I went back to school for a career change. I now live and work in Chicago. How are you? I know that your husband recently passed. I know how hard that can be. I lost my husband also five years ago."

There's that term again, she briefly thought. She nearly wanted to ask, "Where did you lose him?" But she refrained.

The voice of her stylist threw her momentarily. She'd expected someone young and carefree. Not a voice of a confident business woman. "You did? Oh my goodness, you sound so young too."

"It was cancer. I at least had some warning, though I'm not so sure the warning prepared me for his death. But that's not why we're calling today. Let's get you fitted. I'm sure you are as sick as I was of hearing condolences. Time to move on. Am I right?"

She was starting to like this woman. Though blunt as she was. "Yes, although I'm not really sure of my current size. I've lost some weight recently. Right now I'm mostly interested in basics like a nice pair of black straight-leg trousers. I've got a list for you if that's possible."

She heard a little typing while she was on the phone with her, knowing the stylist was putting her stated information into some kind of database.

"Sure, what I'll do is send you a few sizes. What is your ball-park trouser size, please?"

"Well, I used to wear a size eight, but I believe I'm around a size six or possibly a four now, and I usually wear a medium, but some smalls fit as well."

"Yes, different designers have their own sizes it seems. They are *not* standardized. Let's start off with a pair of Theory trousers. I'll send a few sizes. If you send me your list, I'll get started on your box. If you ever have any questions, you can text me directly through the app or call my number. If you have any special occasions coming up, you can let me know that as well. All of our items arrive with a free return label. Just put the returns back into the same box with the return label, and the app will automatically send a pickup service to your address to pick it up. All you have to do is put the box out in front of your door on pickup day. It's really simple."

"Well, I tell you, this has really saved me."

The stylist was silent for a second. "I know what it's like to suddenly be alone. I lost my husband right after our son moved out to college. I went from making dinner for three to trying to figure out how to live utterly alone. It's a journey, but it doesn't have to be a painful one. Having a new wardrobe is something that will make you learn your new identity as an independent woman. I used to live my life for my son and husband. Now, I'm my own person. If you don't do this, move on, it's just not healthy, Vivienne. I've seen what happens when a spouse does not move on, does not grow into their own individual. It's a madness I wouldn't wish on anyone. Live, grow, and become who you are. It's your time now. Let nothing stand in your way. I'm sure your husband would want this for you."

She chuckled a little to herself. "I'm not sure what Todd would want for me now. He was so overprotective. He loved me of course. I know he would want me to be happy; he wouldn't want me to suffer. So, yes, I think this is what he'd want for me. Thank you. I'm choosing to have good days now. So talking to you has helped. Thank you very much."

"My pleasure. I'll keep in touch, Vivienne. Let me know when you get the box, and be specific about what you like and don't like. Tell the truth, no more appeasing anyone else but you."

"I'll do that. Thanks again. Bye."

She ended the call. It was midafternoon, and the fall breeze was picking up a few desiccated leaves from the lawn, playing with them in the air before they descended once again. She wanted to go for a walk, but her heel was throbbing since that morning, and when she'd unwrapped it, the red ring around the wound was brighter and more painful than the night before. So her next call was to her physician, Dr. Thomas.

She made an appointment for later that day since they'd had a cancellation that morning, and it worked out perfectly. It gave her just enough time to drive through the packed rush-hour traffic of Seattle to arrive on time. The only problem was that her phone kept buzzing with text messages, and when traffic slowed to a crawl, she looked at her phone momentarily to see that her son was becoming increasingly worried as to why she hadn't returned his call or text.

"Ta! He'll just have to wait." She wasn't about to break the cardinal rule of texting while driving.

When she finally arrived in the parking lot, she sent him a quick message: "I'm fine. I'm at the doctor's office. No worries. Will call later. Love, Mom."

By the time she checked in at the front office, Brian had sent another text, now frantic. "What do you mean at the doctor's? What happened?"

"Nothing. I cut my heel. Having it looked at. I'm all right."

"Where are you?"

"Dr. Thomas's office. I'm fine. Call later."

She didn't hear a response after that. The nurse called her back, and she sat on the crisp sterile paper atop the table for a few minutes before Dr. Thomas came in. The first thing out of his mouth was, "Vivienne, I'm so sorry to hear about Todd's passing."

She smiled sympathetically. "Yes, it's been a tough few months. It'll be six weeks soon."

"How are you coping?"

She nodded as he pulled a little stool between his legs and sat down in front of her. She'd always found his big bushy, dark eyebrows a bit intimidating. Like two caterpillars that might escape at any minute and creep down to the floor, loose and on the hunt for a new host.

"I'm OK. I just broke a glass jar on the patio and a shard went through the sole of my moccasin. I thought the cut was healing, but it's a bit red now." She was doing her best to deflect questions about her mourning her dead husband.

He nodded, catching on to her rebound. It was as if the man could see through her. His perception was unnerving, but Todd had liked Dr. Thomas, and so she'd always gone to him for non-female-related ailments too.

"Well, let's take a look then." He wrapped his newly washed fingers around the backside of her ankle, slid her black flat off her foot, and took off the wound's bandage to examine the cut. "Yeah, you got a little infection going on here. Nothing to worry about though. I'll clean it up and redress the wound, but you'll need to do a course of antibiotics. Then call me if it's not cleared up by the time you finish the medication. Had you come in when this happened, I would have suggested stitches. Now this will have to heal on its own. Try not to wait so long next time. At least when this scars it's not in a place that matters much."

He'd begun assembling items needed to clean the wound when he asked, "So, how are you feeling? All right otherwise? Coping with Todd's death? Do you think you might need antidepressants? It's not a shame. I know how close you and Todd were."

She knew he'd ask that question eventually, and she was prepared with an answer. "Really, I'm fine. Living without him is certainly a learning experience, but I'm OK. I have good days and bad now." She was doing her best to keep a smile on her face. To reassure this man that had known them both but was certainly closer to Todd than herself.

"Are you considering going back to work? You painted, right?"

"I'm thinking about it. I might get a dog. I might go and visit Izzy in Paris. I just haven't decided yet."

He put astringent along her cut, which stung initially. She jumped slightly. "I'm sorry. I should have warned you. It'll be over in a second," he said, and he was right. The stinging subsided quickly, and he placed a new bandage on the injury. "It should mend well. But keep an eye out for redness, and don't walk on it." He laughed, knowing the absurdity of the request. "Just try to walk on the ball of your foot if you can get away with it."

"I will. I've had some practice with that lately. Thank you."

As he cleaned his hands again, he said, "Vivienne, I've known you and Todd for going on twenty years or more it seems. Todd and I served on a few community boards together. He loved you very much. I'm sure he'd want you to be happy. Don't suffer in silence." He reached into his lab coat and pulled a card from his shirt pocket. "Here's my personal number. If you need anything. Please call me. If you just need to talk, I'm here for you."

She wasn't sure what to think as he handed her his number. She had to scramble for his first name through her memory bank; she finally found it without too much delay. "Thank you, Mark.

I'm really doing fine. It's day by day. I feel like I'm making progress."

He nodded. When she stood he hugged her. "Don't be a stranger," he said, and left the room. She watched the white lab coat walk away and then found her purse and went out into the lobby as carefully as she could walk. What surprised her when she opened the door was her son, Brian, sitting in the waiting room while fumbling with his phone, dressed in his customary suit and tie.

"Brian!" She couldn't believe he was standing there in the waiting room.

"Mom, how's your foot?" he asked, and came to stand beside her as if she was gravely injured.

"I told you; it's fine. There's no need for you to come all the way over here. Really, it was just a cut that got a little infected."

The nurse sitting at the desk watched the banter back and forth.

"I was worried."

"I told you it was nothing."

"Still, how are you going to drive home? You should have called me or Katherine. We could have come and taken you."

She put her hand on his arm. "Brian, there's no need for that. It's just a little injury. Nothing to worry about. Dr. Thomas took care of it. I have a prescription for antibiotics, and he cleaned it up. Nothing to worry about."

"That's a relief," he said, running a worried hand through his hair, "but why didn't you tell me? You need to tell me these things."

"Brian...it's a small thing. Nothing you needed to be alerted to. That's very kind of you to care for me so much, but truly, I'm not going to bother you or Katherine over something like this."

He lowered his voice. "Mother, you are never a bother to us. Please don't feel that way."

She smiled but let out a slightly frustrated breath. It seemed nothing she could say would convince him that she was all right. "Everything is OK now. No need to drive me home. I can still walk perfectly fine. How about we grab some lunch so your trip out here wasn't completely for nothing?"

She smiled at the nurse and then quickly signed the necessary insurance document she offered with the pen she'd been holding out to her. How was it she could communicate with a complete stranger with only a smile and a nod, but no matter what she said to her son, he could not get her meaning with her carefully placed words? He was really starting to remind her of Todd in the early years.

Later they found themselves seated in a nearby café. She ordered the Cobb salad, and he ordered the club sandwich with a side of Ivar's famous clam chowder.

"How is work going?"

He wiped his mouth with a napkin and sat the wedge of sandwich from which he had just taken a bite down on the edge of his plate. "It's fine. This new case is a pain."

She knew he wasn't telling her everything since it seemed he'd taken over the role of caretaker in their relationship. But behind those worried eyes she saw stress. Her son was so much like his father it was uncanny. He favored her more in looks, with her dark-blond hair and facial structure, but Brian was his father's son through and through. "Take time to relax, Brian," she said, and placed a hand over his. He looked up at her, and she smiled.

"It's hard without Dad."

It was the only admission she knew she would obtain from him. "Of course, but you know your dad had complete faith in you, son."

He nodded but didn't say a word. He was having a moment, and she thought if he tried to speak, he might just break down, and she wouldn't encourage that in public. She let go of his hand, and he brought his napkin to his eyes and then took a deep breath.

"I swear it hasn't hit me until recently that he's not coming back."

"I stare at his office door from my office, expecting him to walk out any minute. They haven't even taken his nameplate down yet. I don't think anyone wants to be responsible for touching it."

She nodded in understanding then. They were all mourning Todd's loss. He'd touched so many lives.

"How are the children?" she asked, to give him an opportunity to change the subject.

"Oh, they're great." He grinned like he was about to laugh out loud. "Katherine has Sybil learning a new song at bedtime. Something about a firefly. And she pushes her tush up into the air at the end."

"Katherine?"

Brian laughed out loud so hard that the nearby patrons looked their way.

"No! Sybil."

She'd known it was Sybil but was doing her best to lighten her son's mood—and what a better way? It was evident to her how much he loved his family, and she was proud of him and his decisions.

"Have you heard from Izzy?"

"Yes, she's set me up with a stylist, and I've gone through my wardrobe to update it and renew things."

"Oh, sounds like fun. Not."

"It's a girl thing. I need a few projects to keep me moving from one day to the next."

"That's good, Mom. Something to keep you busy."

"I think I'll start selling my old clothes online."

"Oh, Mom, you don't have to do that. Just give them to charity. You have plenty to live on. I've done all the paperwork. You don't have anything to worry about. Dad made sure you were taken care of."

"I know that, but I want to. I'd like to use what I earn from them to help pay for the new things. I like recycling things. Old into new. That's how I look at it."

"You don't need to work or anything."

"Now that you mention it, I...might go back to the gallery. Michelle said she'd be happy to have me teaching whenever I was ready."

"Why don't you start painting again?"

She signed. "I have. I went out last night on the boat and had a lovely session with the sunset. I'll probably keep doing that. It brings me peace."

"How are the paintings?"

"You have to want to paint. They're OK. Not great, yet. I'm just not feeling my old self yet. I hope more inspiration comes in time, but I don't know what's holding me back."

More nodding as he munched on a string french fry.

"I understand, but I don't want to see you *working* in the gallery."

"I like teaching there. Michelle and the others were my friends. There are many talented people there, and I enjoy spending time with them."

"Why weren't they at Dad's funeral then?"

"I don't know, Brian. It's not like we keep up with those circles anymore. Maybe they never heard about his death. I certainly didn't tell them. I haven't been in the gallery in some time. In fact, I've really let that relationship slide, I guess. I was so busy with your father and our life. The last time I spoke to Michelle, it was last year when I ran into her at an exhibit I dragged your dad to."

She smiled at the memory, and Brian seemed a little more settled.

"I want you to be happy, Mom. I just don't want you to take too many chances, driving all over in this city in this crazy traffic."

"Hey, who taught you to drive? I'm a perfectly good driver," she said, trying to ease his worry.

He chuckled. "You did. Dad was too busy back then."

"Yeah, make time for the family."

"Oh, I'm not resentful. He had a lot to do. Well, I've got to get back to the office," he said as he looked at his watch. "You sure you don't want me to drive you home and have someone pick up your car?"

"I'm positive. I can drive home perfectly fine on my own. I'm going to stop off at the pharmacy to pick up my prescription on the way. Don't worry about me."

"I have to, Mom. The baton's been passed. Text me when you get home so I don't worry. I love you." He kissed her on the temple, and they left to their separate cars. She was thankful that he left the parking lot first so that she didn't feel like he was watching as she drove, critiquing her every move like Todd had often done.

"Hmm, I'll have to have a serious talk with him if he keeps this up," she said to herself, and drove back across town.

By the time she pulled into the driveway, she'd debated texting him or not but in the end decided to go ahead and do it this time, knowing he was expecting her to send the confirmation or he'd worry about her and probably try to call her soon. There was no need for that in her mind, so she sent off a quick "I'm here."

Later that evening, she decided to get started on selling her old items online. She hung a simple chrome hook over Isabel's bedroom door, where the afternoon light was the best coming through her bedroom window, and hung the red floral dress she'd worn once to a business dinner years before.

The cut wasn't right for her now. The hemline was too short, and the bright floral was something she'd worn in earlier times but was no longer her style. She used the online selling app on her iPad and simply filled out all the information requested after she took just three photos. First of the front, then a close up of the tag at the back of the neck, and then the last picture of the back. Once the photos were taken, she put in a modest price for auction and pressed complete. The whole process took her less than five minutes.

She looked at all her clothes hanging in Izzy's closet and realized she had a lot of work to do if she wanted to sell them this way. She didn't want to spend all her time listing clothing though, so like the progressive notification list, she decided she'd list five new items a day and let the progress take care of itself.

After she had completed the listing for the fifth item of the day, she found that she already had five watchers on the first dress she listed. "By this time next week, I might have sales." Then she realized she'd need shipping envelopes and shipping labels, so she shopped in her favorite online store and quickly purchased them. She was a major customer for household items and knew the items she ordered would arrive in at least two days' time. "Easy peasy," she said to herself.

Checking her e-mail she saw that she'd received a nice message from her stylist, Veronica, thanking her for her trust in picking out items for her and asking her to look over the box she'd assembled. Vivienne clicked on the app, and there was a notice for her to look in her wardrobe and approve the items being sent. "I didn't realize you could see the items ahead of time. That's so cool." Then she felt a little ridiculous. "I'm going to have to get a pet if I continue to talk to myself."

There were at least fifteen items in the box. The first three were the same trousers they'd spoke about in three different sizes. Then there was a white silk blouse, three black dresses, a full black skirt, a striped shirt, a lovely structured khaki trench coat, a pair of leopard flats that she wasn't too sure about but would give a try at least, and a black blazer, along with a few pairs of jeans and a few scarves. "Wow, she didn't waste any time." There wasn't anything that she truly didn't like, and even though she wasn't too sure about the leopard flats, she could see herself wearing them with jeans and her black turtleneck, so she clicked the accept button. Another screen flashed, saying her items were on their way. "Well, how about that?"

Her next mission was to tidy the house a bit and get to sleep earlier in hopes that she could reset her internal clock to make herself wake at an earlier hour, but when she passed by her studio room door on her way to her bedroom and saw her easel standing in the shadow of late-afternoon light, she stopped and stared inside. The canvas she started on the Puget Sound sat there incomplete, with a beautiful sunset lined by an indigo horizon. She had a long way to go before it was complete and worthy for anyone's eyes. Though today she wasn't venturing out to the sound. There were too many firsts in this day, and her heel hurt a little too much. No, she would take it easy this evening and hopefully feel inspired to work on the canvas soon.

A dusty-blue hue cast through the shade she had drawn closed in the room. The canvas called to her, but she didn't see anything in the emptiness to prompt her to finish. That's what she told herself anyway. "Maybe tomorrow," she said as if it were a promise to fulfill.

❧ 19 ❧

P resent
      Lake Union, Washington

WHILE SIPPING TEA AT THE GRANITE COUNTERTOP AND
checking over the items that had sold in the last online auction,
the doorbell rang. When she checked the door, the mail truck
was pulling away, and found the packages he'd left on her
doorstep. She'd received the labels as well as the envelopes and
had watched the auction action as the items ended. Some of them
had several bids, and only a few only had a single bid. Seems her
items were indeed in demand. There was only one item that she
had to relist at a lower price in hopes that it would sell the
following week along with the new items she'd listed.

She also had several questions about her listings and spent a
lot of time going back and taking measurements and noted that in
her next listings she'd include the measurements in the description instead of winging it. She could list five items easily from

start to finish in half an hour so that the task didn't become too daunting each day.

Along with the other packages on the doorstep, a large brown cardboard cube sat right in front of her on her doormat.

"Wow," she said. The box was so large there was a brown plastic handle affixed to the top of the box. She simply picked up the box by the handle as if it were a piece of luggage and brought the package inside. After cutting the tape with scissors, she unfolded the top lid and inside were bundles of neatly folded clothing and articles from her stylist. Vivienne knew the box was coming but hadn't kept abreast of when the package would arrive. Each bundle was wrapped in white cloth tape, holding the items together firmly so that they wouldn't jostle around. However, on top was a silver envelope, and inside was a note from Veronica explaining each piece, an invoice, and a return label with two more pieces of precut sticky tape for the return items.

"They think of everything. How cool is this?" she said, and pulled out the first bundle of items with the cream silk blouse stacked on top of a few other items. She pulled the tie loose and unfolded the shirt. Not only was it beautiful, she knew it would go with almost everything she already owned as well as the many new items she would soon own.

Almost giddy with excitement, she brought the new clothes into her bedroom and began laying them out on her neatly made bed. She undressed and tried on each piece, finding that the size six slacks fit her the best now. "Well, I can finally get rid of the other baggy ones then. She put on the silk blouse and tucked the remaining fabric into the waistband of the black slacks and then glanced down at her bare feet. She remembered the shoe box on her bed and pulled out the questionable leopard flats by Seychelles. She tried on the pointy flats and walked around in front of her full-length mirror.

In the reflection was a look she'd never thought to try before but found that she liked the sophistication of. A little more refined is what she felt with the subtle leopard flats. She reached for one of the solid cashmere-blend scarves and chose the black one with a basket weave texture, wondering if it would be too much with the leopard print. To her surprise the outfit looked perfectly chic.

"I think I do like these shoes." The outfit was a classic look that she could wear practically anywhere, not only to do normal errands on a weekday but also go to a gallery event. In an outfit like this, she could even meet her son for lunch, for that matter. The ensemble was refreshingly versatile.

She then tried on the dresses and found the size six fit her perfectly again. This time with the solid-black ponte-knit dress, she wore black heels and the printed bright floral silk scarf by Ted Baker, and the jewel tones made all the difference. "Definitely a fancier outfit." Then she tried the same dress with a polka-dot silk scarf and her black flats and found the look more casual to wear for a luncheon or a day with the grandgirls.

Once everything was tried on, she decided that only the redundant sizes that proved too big or too small would go back, so she wrapped those items back up in the twill cording they'd arrived in and placed them back in the box, affixed the new tapes to secure the opening, and then hung up all her new clothing from dark to light and in sections from blouses to dresses.

Then she hauled the large cube box containing the returns back out to the front door and left it inside. She opened the stylist app and filled out the checkout information, saying what she did and did not like about each item. And then a shipping notification popped up, and she selected a pickup-date request for the next day. Remembering what Isabel had told her about the process, she said, "It's that easy." And it was.

"I better get those sold items packaged and off to their new owners." Going back to Izzy's room, she printed out the labels she needed and carefully folded the sold items in tissue paper and slid them into the mailing envelopes. Once she was finished, she carried those packages too out to the front door and scheduled a pickup with the post office online. She loved not having to go anywhere with this whole process. She could buy and sell items from her home. And she'd already paid for half of her new purchases. It was a completely gas-free experience.

After placing them by the door, she turned around and looked at her house. "Five-bedroom home...and just one resident." She started to examine all the contents of the large Lake Union house as she slowly walked through the museum-like formal living room and dining room.

Rattling around inside such a large empty house was beginning to drain her. She wasn't sure what to do about the situation; there were so many memories in every room she looked. Christmases in the formal living room, with them all in their pajamas drinking hot cocoa with wrapping paper everywhere. Thanksgiving dinner in the formal dining room of years past. The time the cranberry sauce fell to the floor before it ever reached the table. All of those memories still lingered like ghosts as she walked through the rooms each time.

Since the house was a coveted piece of property, there was no way she'd sell, but perhaps she'd approach Brian to see if he'd like to own the estate himself and live there with his young family. That was an inspiring option but one she'd keep to herself for now and think about at a later time. After all, she wasn't sure where she'd move to yet.

Her thoughts were interrupted by her phone vibrating. She retrieved it off the kitchen counter and checked to see who was calling. Seeing Isabel's number, she answered without hesitation.

"Hi, Mom. I got your message about the new clothes Veronica sent to you. How do you like them?"

"I *love* them. It's so refreshing to have new items in my closet that I know I'll wear every day."

"You have to send me pictures."

She let out a little embarrassed laugh. "I can't take pictures of myself...I'll try, maybe. She sent three pairs of the same black trousers, and they're perfect. I love everything she sent. The only things I returned were the items with redundant sizes. Oh, Izzy, this has really helped me. Thank you for introducing me to her."

"That's wonderful, Mom. Please send pictures. I only called real quickly. I have to meet Armand in a few minutes, so I have to run."

"Oh, trusting me with his name now? Armand? Things are going well then?"

"Yes, Mom."

Vivienne could tell her daughter was blushing through the phone.

"I'll introduce you to him when you come to visit."

"I would love to meet him, Izzy."

"OK, sorry I have to go now. Love you. Bye, Mom."

"Bye, darling."

Vivienne ended the call. She looked around again. A memory of a young Isabel ran past her, barefoot and dressed in a flannel nightgown, her brown hair unruly. "Oh Todd...I wish you were here," Vivienne said as she hung up.

❧ 20 ❧

P resent
Lake Union, Washington

A WEEK LATER, VIVIENNE FOUND HERSELF ROAMING AROUND the empty house again after setting another load of outgoing auction parcels by the front door for the post office to pick up the next day, when her phone buzzed.

"Hello?"

"Hi, Vivienne, it's Michelle from the Frank Museum. Remember me?"

Vivienne's first thought was that they too were going to offer their condolences, and she just wasn't quite up to that today. She hadn't put up her defenses yet that morning. She'd barely slept the night before out of sheer boredom and instead stayed up half the night researching flights to Paris in case she thought about taking Isabel up on her offer.

"Oh course, Michelle. I remember you. It's only been since

last year. How are things? Sorry, I've been out of the loop for so long now."

"Yes, we've missed you here. That's actually why I'm calling. We're hoping you're interested in coming back to do a few workshops for a sketching class this season. Our current teacher is on maternity leave, and we need someone to temporarily pick up a few of her sketch workshop classes."

"Oh," Vivienne said in surprise that condolences were not the reason for the call after all. "Well, what's the schedule? I do have some free time coming, but I'm not sure I'm up for anything permanent right now."

"Well, let's meet this week and maybe we can go over the schedule. You were the first pick from the staff and students as the temporary replacement. Our students still ask for you."

"Really? Wow, that's nice to know. I haven't really done a lot of work lately. My husband recently passed away."

"Oh my gosh, I'm *so sorry* to hear that, Vivienne," Michelle said. An empty space of time elapsed between them before she quickly injected, "Are you sure you're up to taking this on?"

"Oh, yes...my goodness. I've been walking around this house alone for too long now. I think teaching would be good for me, honestly. It's just a few hours a week, anyway. No, I think it's good timing with a temporary commitment. Would you like me to meet you at the studio?"

"Yes, could you come by on Wednesday, say around noon?"

"Yes, of course. That's perfect. I'll look forward to meeting with you then. Have a good evening, and thank you for thinking of me again."

"You're doing us a huge favor. I'll see you then. Bye now."

After the call, Vivienne went right into her studio without waiting for the canvas to invite her over the threshold and opened the window, pulling the shade up and letting the soft light of late morning cascade inside and filled the room with a natural brilliance.

She sat on the stool in front of the canvas and picked up her sketch pencil without having an idea. She just began to draw what came to her, pushing the ideas to come. She sat back after a while and gazed at what she'd done. The lighting had changed, and she realized she must have spent a couple of hours sitting there. She sat her pencil down, rose from her stool, and placed her hands on her lower back and stretched. It was as if she were possessed, driven even, by some unknown force. A force she hadn't felt in a very long time.

She'd never liked working by artificial light, so she left the room without a glance back into the dimness. Her work, in this way, could marinate in time until it was bright enough to see once again. When the next sunrise came, she'd return to the piece. Maybe the art would show something glorious or prove to need new direction. Whatever the case, her art needed time to saturate the graphite into something wholly different and complete.

❋ 21 ❋

P resent
Seattle, Washington

VIVIENNE ARRIVED A FEW MINUTES EARLY TO THE STUDIO, AND when she did, it was as if she'd never left. The double glass doors invited her inside onto the polished stone flooring. The whole building was designed in a way to mimic nature and the surroundings of the Northwest, which she found relaxing.

Young school students on a field trip were gathered in the foyer with their guide. Their chatter reminding Vivienne of long ago days chaperoning her own children and their classmates on such events. Vivienne smiled when she spotted Michelle coming her way over the children's heads. She waited until the tour guide led the class away like a school of fish following their chosen leader.

Vivienne wasn't certain why she'd stopped coming and signing up for more classes to teach. Too busy with Todd and his activities perhaps was the reason. He never liked for her to go anywhere on her own, and he'd often call or text her when she was there, making her feel as if he resented her time away. Maybe she'd just given up and conceded to his need to hover over her in time. It didn't matter now. She was back, and seeing Michelle greet her near the entrance, she felt in a way she belonged there teaching and enjoying the creative vibe.

"Hi, Vivienne! I'm so glad you came," Michelle said, and embraced her.

"I'm happy to be here."

"You look great!"

Vivienne chose to wear her black slacks with the cream silk blouse and leopard flats. She felt confident and ready for something new.

"Thank you. So do you."

"Well, come into my office, and we can discuss the details." Michelle led her down the stone path past the gift shop to her office. Along the way, Vivienne looked along the walls at the current exhibits, fascinated by all the changes she'd missed in the recent years.

"I'm so excited you're going to sub for Melody. She's due any day now, but her doctor put her on bed rest early. She's expecting *twins*," Michelle said with glee.

Michelle was the type of woman who had a perpetual smile on her face. Time had not changed that. Vivienne often thought perhaps she took a lot of extra B12 or something but was too afraid to ask. She had more energy than a four-year-old after a big slice of birthday cake.

"Well, this is perfect timing for me. I need something to do while I'm preparing to take a trip to France later this year to visit my daughter, and I'm cleaning out the house in the meantime."

"France? Isabel's in France? We have a lot to catch up on. Then I called at the right moment. I love it when things come together like this with perfect timing. Still, I'm sorry to hear about your husband." She stopped and laid a consoling hand on Vivienne's forearm.

Vivienne nodded. She knew she shouldn't have brought up Todd's death in the phone conversation, though she didn't feel like breaking down any longer. "Grieving is a process. I'm fine. Actually, I should say, I'm getting there."

Michelle's kind eyes stared into her for a time. "I lost my mother a few years ago." She took a breath and let it out slowly. "I couldn't even order Chinese takeout without breaking down on the phone for weeks. It was the hardest thing I've ever been through. You're right; sometimes we have to keep going despite how we feel. Life's too hard otherwise." She continued to her office at the end of the hall.

The room was cramped, with a desk covered in papers taking up most of the space. Vivienne thought it funny how those who typically were artistic were also messy individuals. Once they were seated, Michelle handed Vivienne the class schedule to look over, and she calculated how long the car trip would take her to get to the class from her end of town and then what time she would arrive home in the evenings. "The classes run from two to four Tuesdays and Thursdays and five to seven on Saturdays. That should give me enough time to arrive home without driving in the dark for too long this time of year."

"Oh, it will be pitch black this time of year after four in the evening. Will that be a problem?"

"Oh no, I don't think so. It's not forever."

"And there are six classes total. Do you see any that you potentially might not be able to teach? We can always call in a student teacher. Just let us know beforehand."

Vivienne scanned the requirements and the schedule again. She'd actually helped develop the very same classes years ago. "No, it all looks very doable. I think it will work out great."

"Oh, wonderful. Melody, our current teacher, hasn't changed

anything since you left. The syllabus is still the same, so I think the instruction is pretty straight forward."

"Perfect. Then I look forward to getting started."

Michelle stood, and Vivienne did as well as a close to their meeting. "Well, I'm really looking forward to having you in there. It'll keep some of our students from continuously asking for you. You know, if you decide you'd like to come back permanently, let us know. We can always work you into different classes."

"Oh, thank you. Baby steps for me for now. I don't want to commit to anything permanent quite yet."

They shook hands, and Vivienne was soon on her way back. She looked forward to teaching next week and getting started. Before leaving, she checked out the classroom and inventory of all of the supplies. Everything was essentially as she'd left it years ago. So there was nothing more for her to pick up or arrange for.

She'd put the schedule into the calendar app on her phone, and for some reason having those classes to teach and look forward to gave her another purpose and a new reason for waking up for each day.

❧ 22 ❧

P resent
Lake Union, Washington

"BUT I WANT TO WORK, BRIAN. IT'S GOOD FOR ME TO HAVE more to do."

She couldn't believe she was having this phone conversation with her son. Why didn't he understand that she couldn't just roam around the house all the time doing nothing?

"I just don't think it's a good idea to drive all the way over there just for a few hours three days a week," Brian said.

"Brian. This is something I want to do. There's no reason to hold me back, and it's only temporary. I feel like I'm *asking* for your permission," she said, with a chuckle. "When did you become the boss of me?" She meant it as a rhetorical question in a lighthearted tone, but the silence dragged on a heartbeat too long. "Brian?"

"Mom, you have everything you need there. Can't you find

something local? That trip is nearly an hour drive each way with this traffic. And it will be pitch dark by the time you get home."

"Brian, I'll be fine. Thank you for the concern. The real reason for my call though was Katherine's upcoming birthday. Do you have any plans yet? What do you think she'd like?"

"Changing the subject, I see. Fine. I haven't really thought about what to get her yet. I'll ask her tonight. I'm sure we'll have dinner somewhere or do something at home. I'll let you know, but I need to go. I've got a meeting in two minutes."

"OK, have a good day, son," she said, but he'd already left, and with the frustrated tone of not getting his way. It saddened her to disagree with her children on occasion, but they needed to learn that she had a life to live as well.

Even though Brian was only trying to keep her safe, as his father had done, it was a stifling kind of caring, and she needed to desperately shake free of those bonds or she'd go insane trying to keep herself entertained in the large house she'd come at times to regard as a personal prison, no matter the lovely furnishings. Seeing the way he reacted to her new activity, she wondered how he was going to take her going to visit Isabel in Paris when he found out her plans.

That's when the doorbell rang. She'd heard the familiar sound of the mailman's approach down her long drive to her door. Paying no mind to the routine, there was no need to go to the door. She would only interfere with his day and with the efficient system. This time however, with the many auction package pick-ups, he deposited a delivery.

Vivienne had known another delivery from Veronica was on the way but wasn't keeping track of which day. This delivery was the second set of new clothes she'd requested for her French wardrobe, and now that she knew what to expect, it was like Christmas morning.

In this delivery she was most excited about the evening clutch options that were chosen for her. Among the other items, Vivienne asked for a neutral or metal-tone evening clutch, something that would go with everything. She'd busily sold the many bags she'd already owned on the auctions site, and the striped bags, pastel clutches, pleather and leather ones were all happily traded for one perfect clutch. The concept of paring down to the most quality item afforded appealed to her. The more she accomplished this, the more she knew this was the right way to go. There was no need for fifteen purses in various shapes and sizes and of any imaginable hue. There was only a need for a nice evening clutch, a black leather bag, a brown leather bag, and a leather tote. Today, she would choose the perfect clutch.

Among the choices was a light-gold leather option by Kate Spade New York. It came with a detachable strap so that it could be worn as a cross-body bag as well. The duplicity was appealing. She tried it on over her shoulder while standing in front of the mirror. It was a light-gold tone, had one opening flap, and was well enough made.

The second contender was a Michael Kors silver Saffiano leather cross-body bag. This one sported a chain as a detachable handle. She liked the understated silver, though the pale gold of the previous one wasn't ostentatious by any measure. The chain strap fell into place over her shoulder easily. The thought occurred to her that it could also be used as a weapon if accosted in a dark alley. She chuckled at the idea wielding the chain like a wild woman in defense from a would-be attacker.

Then she picked up the third option. This clutch was like the pale-gold tone of the first, but it had a fold-over opening sometimes referred to as an envelope clutch. The leather reminded her of her mother's old leather bags; there was a thick heft to the clutch. There was no shoulder strap included, making it a true clutch bag. And the opening had a dual metal bar attached in a pewter and a gold tone. She liked the combination together.

When she opened the clutch, it smelled of leather and had a beautiful gold silk lining inside. This one was by Diane von Furstenberg, and of the three, this one was the winner for Vivienne. It embodied everything she wanted in a clutch bag and, as a bonus, the purse reminded her of her mother's but in a modern design. The craftsmanship was superb, and she couldn't imagine a better choice.

In the old days, she would have possibly kept the silver one as well, but those days were over. She wanted one well-made item to take up precious space in her life and nothing more. There was no need to fill a closet to the brim, and this would do perfectly.

Each clutch came with its own maker's protective cloth bag, and she refolded the two returns carefully and laid them into the return box.

She also received a camel cashmere twin sweater set which included the softest cardigan and shell she'd ever felt. She changed into a new pair of dark strait-leg jeans and tried the sweater set on. Her fawn-toned hair cascaded down to her shoulders. Included in the delivery were also a pair of Cognac leather short boots with an inside zipper, so she slipped those on with the denim and stood in front of the mirror. She loved the way the cashmere felt against her skin, as if this fiber were what humans should have been born into, the softness was so compelling. She added her pearl earrings and matching pearl necklace to the outfit and looked again in the mirror. Vivienne loved the outfit, knowing she could wear the ensemble practically anywhere.

Then, she tried the sweater set with the black pencil skirt and black pumps she obtained in the last shipment, and again the tops worked perfectly. She loved the clever rules of this wardrobe system, knowing she needed to choose her items wisely so that each piece could be worn many different ways. She picked up the clutch and wore it under her arm, checking all angles. In all, after she'd tried everything on, she chose to return three items that didn't fit the rules because they were either a color or a print she just didn't need. After giving them a good try despite the rules, they failed to prove as versatile, and she knew they'd end up sitting in her closet without being worn enough. Those were decisions she'd passed by and never wanted to return to again.

She carefully packed up the returns and hung the new items in her closet. Seeing her options expand gave her a sense of fulfillment. Her closet was now a curated one, one she chose for herself carefully and with a purpose. It was one more step into having control of her own life and its new direction.

The next morning, after going through her morning routine, Vivienne placed the outgoing parcels on her porch as usual. When she returned, she passed by the formal living room, a room she rarely entered anymore. Brian often joked that it was a museum, and it was. The air nearly stagnate inside, she opened a window.

Yesterday marked the end of the items to sell in Isabel's closet. At first she thought that would be the end of her adventure into ridding herself of the things she didn't need. Now she found herself wandering the house to see what was next. And further, why could she not devote the same process as the French wardrobe to the rest of her home?

The concept would remain the same. Only have what is necessary. Each and every item needed to be cherished, or it would go, plain and simple. There was no need to hoard things in one's life just to take up space in the name of memories. In doing so, it only held you down, held you back to remain in a kind of prison of your own making.

Knowing she had only a few days before she started work at the art museum, Vivienne grabbed her iPad once again and set to work. She listed everything from tiny crystal creatures to floral tapestries hung on the walls and porcelain vases she didn't even know she owned or where they had come from in the first place.

She cleaned out cupboards, desks, and end tables and then

listed them for sale as well. She worked all morning and then went to work, and when she returned in the evening, she answered questions online from those interested in the items she had for sale. She packaged items carefully and shipped them off, and before long she found the house lighter, clearer, and uncluttered with minutia. The effect pleased her.

On the evenings she didn't work, she took the boat out on Puget Sound. She brought along her canvas and continued to sketch and paint each evening and began to even pack her dinner and a thermos of tea so she could leave earlier and stay longer out at sea. Each night, she'd return with a refreshed spirit. She also began to walk in the mornings after she'd packaged up her auctions, waving hello to neighbors along her route. With her new activities, she began to feel stronger and more capable than she'd been before, and she also realized she wasn't nearly as afraid of the things she once was.

As much as she loved Todd, she'd realized his neurosis rubbed off on her in ways she hadn't imagined. Once when she was out walking along the narrow road, she remembered him often saying, "I'm *afraid* for you to do this or that." He'd always used the term "I'm afraid." And then one day, she was scared of traveling alone to the grocery store. Or of taking a walk alone in the evening. Of breathing too deeply or daring too far.

"Oh, Todd," she said as she stared into another glorious sunset. How she loved him wasn't ever a question. She'd do it all again; only a little more defiant this time. A little more willpower. She hoped he didn't live in the dark more than she knew of. The thought saddened her. She scuffed the gravel as she walked further home. A neighbor passed, and she waved without taking heed of his attention as she would have in the past. He lived here, and so did she, in their own spaces. She breathed in air in a way she had never before. It filled every crevice of her lungs and gave her a strength she'd longed for before.

When she went inside, she called Brian and asked him and

Katherine to come visit her the next week. She'd tell him of her plans to visit Isabel in Paris then and possibly bring up the plans she had for the house as well. Perhaps they could come to some agreement. She'd made up her mind. She was going to Paris, and she was moving on.

�֍ 23 ֍

M ay 15, 1989
     Seattle, Washington
     The Mathis House

"TODD, CAN YOU WATCH IZZY?" SHE YELLED DOWN THE HALL
from the girl's bedroom as the new baby shrieked from hunger, a
wet diaper, or just needing to be held. She hadn't assessed the
situation yet.

"Yes, I'm coming," Todd said. He'd barely made it in the front
door before Vivienne was already calling to him for help. How did
she handle them all day? He wondered but never voiced the
concern. "Izzy, come see Daddy," he beckoned to her. "She's in the
bathtub, Todd. Can you come sit with her while I take care of
the baby?"

"Oh, sure, just let me set my stuff down." Todd dropped his
briefcase and jacket in the foyer of their home on Seattle's south
side and began rolling up his sleeves on his way up to the children's bathroom, where he found Isabel, his two-year-old's face
among a tub of bubbles with more toys than he could count. She

happily played in the water, sticking foam shapes to the sides of the white walls of the tub. "Hi, Daddy." She waved and his heart melted at the sight of his little girl.

In the background the baby still wailed while Vivienne changed his diaper. "How was your day, dear?" she called from the bedroom.

"Same as usual," he said. He made car noises with a red foam shape, crashing into a square and triangle shape Isabel proclaimed as her house.

"No, Daddy!" she shrieked, but laughed. "You silly, Daddy."

"Hey, honey, have you seen my tortoiseshell clip? The one that my grandmother gave me? I can't seem to find it anywhere."

"No, I haven't seen it," he said automatically, and then returned to Izzy, with a blue piece of foam shaped like a truck, pretending it to be an ambulance while making the appropriate emergency sounds.

Vivienne must have comforted Brian because Todd ceased to hear any more crying from his infant son while he played with his daughter. Then Vivienne stepped into the doorway of the bathroom. He glanced at her standing there, holding their son who was now nursing from one exposed breast with gusto, his little hands holding on to each side of her swollen breast. Vivienne's hair was strewn down in untamed layers around her face. She usually kept it up in a loose bun. He assumed Brian had given her a tough time today. And with a two-year-old to keep track of as well, Todd decided long ago he'd rather have a day job. Vivienne was great at mothering though. He'd admired her patience. He could never say he would trade jobs with her in a second.

"Rough day?" he asked.

"No, not really. We had a doctor's appointment today, and we just got off our schedule. Izzy took a late nap, and Brian missed his feeding. Sorry it was chaos when you came through the door, and I haven't had a chance to start dinner yet."

"Heck, let's order pizza. Don't worry about dinner. Why don't you go order? I'll take care of Izzy here. We've got a five-car collision going on anyway."

"OK, she's already clean, just five more minutes. Her pajamas are on the counter." When she smiled at him, the vision knocked him for a loop. Here she was a mess, feeding their son, and obviously the day had gone from bad to worse, yet she handled the stress with ease. He loved her more now than ever.

Later that night, a miracle happened. Both children were sound asleep at the same time. He thought his chances possible when he wrapped his arm around her waist from behind in the kitchen as she bent over to put dishes in the dishwasher. He pulled her close to him, and she had no doubt as to his intentions because she turned around in his arms to face him. He half expected her to feign tiredness, of which she had every right, but she didn't. She kissed him when he pulled her near, and when his hand slipped up to cup her full breast through her white tank top, she didn't nudge away. He took that as a clear signal to launch, so he scooped her up into his arms and down the hall to their bedroom they went. The dishes could wait.

✿ 24 ✿

P **resent**
Seattle, Washington

THE CLASSROOM FULL OF STUDENTS WITH CANVASSES SET ATOP
easels before them was soundless except for the scratching of
pencils or smudge brushes on canvas. She walked between the
rows of easels inspecting each of her student's work. Occasionally
she'd stop and offer a suggestion or two or guide them in shading
techniques. This was the part of the lesson she loved the most,
when her students were left to perform on their own, with only
her teachings to go by, and proved to themselves a new skill to use
in their own art. It was like passing a shared secret, like a part of
herself. It was a great feeling to see their success, like passing
a baton.

By the time she made the rounds and returned to her desk,
her phone was lit up with a new message. She checked the
message quickly, seeing it was Isabel returning her call and naturally excited that she was committing to the trip to Paris.

After class was over, she planned to race home and slide a lasagna into the oven to get ready for the dinner tonight with her son and Katherine. She wasn't apprehensive about the dinner as much as she thought she would be. Vivienne was confident that she was going to make the trip to Paris. She'd never felt stronger and realized it oddly started with reshaping her wardrobe, which was a minor thing, but the decision making had snowballed into the rest of her life. Now she worked part time, lived alone, and was making plans for the future. Of course she missed Todd, but without him, she had to remake herself or she had little chance to survive, let alone thrive. And that was how she felt now. She was doing more than waking and wandering through her days until sleep finally stopped evading her. She was living again.

"All right, class, we have five more minutes. You can begin packing up. We will start off where we stopped next session. Remember to bring your putty erasers next time; we don't want to erase the entire first layer, just soften the lines."

A few of her students began packing up while the others hurriedly applied a last few loose hand lines. She knew the incessant pull to complete what you set out to do was nearly impossible to abate, but unfortunately they were given limited time in the studio. Some of her students were elderly and took these kinds of classes to break up the mundane parts of life. Many of them were widowed like herself. A few of her students were middle aged, possibly trying to fulfill a deep need to learn the craft, and just a few were moms who wanted to have a few nights out a week. Whatever their reasoning, she was happy to accommodate them.

"Bye, Mrs. Mathis. See you Thursday," one of the young moms dressed in workout clothes said on her way out the door.

Vivienne smiled at her, remembering what it was like to have only a few moments alone when you had a young family, barely enough time to go to the bathroom by yourself. "Yes, I'll see you then," she said, and quickly packed her own demonstrative supplies and headed out the door.

When she pulled up to her driveway, her son and his wife pulled up right behind her. She'd premade the lasagna and only needed to rewarm the casserole for dinner and then toss a salad.

"We almost beat you here," Katherine said.

"Were you running late, Mom?" Brian asked.

"No, I finished up a class and made it just in time. How was your drive over?" she asked, while she let them in the front door.

"We hit a little traffic but nothing major," Brian said.

"That's a relief. You can't go anywhere anymore without it being a whole day trip through the city of Seattle," Vivienne said.

"It seems that way. They fix one route, and it clogs another. That's why Dad was such a proponent of bike riding," Brian said.

The mere mention of his father stabbed her through the heart, and it was apparent by the look on Katherine's face as well. She immediately shot her husband a look of caution. "That probably wasn't the right thing to say," Brian said.

"No, no, you're right. Your dad was always arguing that half of Seattle could bike to their destinations and that there would be so much less traffic congestion and pollution if they did," she said, avoiding eye contact with the two of them and slipping the lasagna in the warm oven.

"What can I do to help you, Vivienne?" Katherine asked while Brian wandered around the house.

"You can help with the salad." Vivienne began to pull items out of the refrigerator, when Brian called her name in slight alarm.

"Mom?"

"Yes?"

"Where's all the stuff from the living room?"

"What do you mean?"

"Your crystal figurines, the picture that used to hang there in the entryway. Are you getting rid of a lot of stuff?"

"Uh, yeah. I thought I'd talk to you guys about some of the changes I'd like to make."

"Changes? What kind of changes? I thought you were happy here."

"Well, I am but I think there're a few things I'd like to alter."

He walked back into the dining room, where she and Katherine were placing the salad and lasagna on the table. "There's a lot of stuff missing. You didn't get ripped off and not tell me, did you?"

They sat down, and Vivienne began to serve the lasagna slices in large rectangles to Brian while Katherine passed the salad around.

"No. I didn't get ripped off. I've been paring down things that I no longer need or feel an attachment to."

"But you don't need to do that, Mom. Dad left you well sustained."

"I know, Brian, but I don't want to use more than is necessary. I like not having so much clutter in the house. In fact, that's why I asked you and Katherine to come to dinner."

She took a sip of her wine. "I've decided to take a trip to Paris and visit with Isabel next month."

Brian looked as if he was choking for a brief second. "What? Alone? Why?" he said, with a scolding tone.

Katherine spoke up to her husband's abrupt question. "Brian, your mom can fly off to see, Izzy. There's no harm in that."

He looked across the table as if insulted by his own wife's audacity to side with his mother. "That's a long trip for her to take on her own, Katherine."

A tense momentary pause lingered, and then Vivienne cut in while Katherine found the food on her plate suddenly quite interesting. "Brian," she ventured, "I'm capable of taking a trip alone. I've traveled by myself in the past, and so has your sister. Please don't act as if I'm helpless."

"Mom, Dad would not want you to take this trip."

"You're probably right," she conceded. "However, I *am* going. And I'll meet your sister on the other side. There's no reasonable explanation for me to not take the trip."

He stared at her in disbelief and took a deep breath out of frustration while shaking his head. "I guess I can't stop you."

She patted the back of his hand. "I'll be fine, Brian. Please don't worry about me."

Then it was Vivienne's turn to take a deep breath. "The other thing I wanted to talk about is...the house."

He'd just taken a large bite of lasagna and fear showed in his eyes suddenly. He began chewing in earnest so that he could object. She started speaking in order to get her point across before he was finished with his bite.

"I think it would be a great opportunity for me to look for something much smaller. It's much too large a space for me alone."

She watched him gulp down his food too soon and followed it with a swallow of water. "Mother. Why didn't you mention this before?"

"I'm telling you now."

"You can't sell this place."

"I didn't say I was going to sell it. I think the house is a great property for the two of you to move into if you'd like to. If you don't want to, I'll consider selling it."

Brian brought his palm to his face. "Are you listening to what you're saying? Dad would be furious. This place is an heirloom. Why don't you want to live here anymore?"

She began a little more carefully. "This is a five-bedroom house. I'm one person, and I need something much smaller now. There are too many memories here, and it's just a waste to keep up the place for one person."

"Dad worked so hard for this house. He wanted this for you."

She turned to Katherine who, at some point, had crossed her legs and was taking bite after bite, listening attentively but was, for the most part, making herself so busy eating she couldn't join in the conversation.

"Your father wanted this place for this family, and now it's just me." She put her napkin on the side of her plate. She was getting tired of him bringing up his father as a defense to keep her in her place. "Brian, I have to live now without your father. I can't do that rambling around in this empty shell of a house. You and Katherine have a growing family. The location is much closer to work, and you're right, it's an heirloom property. No one will be able to purchase a lot like this on Lake Union for a very long time. These houses are being passed down to the next generation. We should keep it in the family. You two should consider moving in here, or I'll consider selling the place."

"Where are you going to live?"

"I haven't decided just yet."

He nodded and took another bite. She knew her son, knew he was thinking over her statements and trying to figure out how he might undermine her decisions. The lawyer in him just couldn't quit looking for an angle that might help him win. Arguing was his career choice. For her part, her tactic was to remain steady and firm in her convictions.

"When are you planning the Paris trip?" Katherine asked, and Brian shot her a trying stare.

"Next month. I e-mailed Izzy the itinerary earlier. I'll talk to her tonight about the rest."

Brian shook his head in frustration but said nothing.

"That's so exciting. I hope we can go someday," her daughter-in-law said, like a shining star. Though Brian didn't like it, not one bit.

"Me too, that would be an excellent adventure for you and the girls," Vivienne ventured to say, though she knew she was pushing it too with the way her son was behaving.

"I don't like it, Mom. You're selling things, you look differ-ent, you're working," he shook his head in disapproval again.

"It's like you don't even...*miss* Dad." He threw his napkin on the table.

Katherine yelled, "Brian!"

"It's true, Katherine. Look at her." He stood and waved his hand at his mother. "She doesn't even *look* the same. I don't even know who you are," he said to Vivienne.

"Brian, calm down. That is *not* true. I love and miss your father obviously far more than you'll ever know. You do not get to accuse *me* of not missing him." She was shaking her finger at him in anger and then pointed at Katherine. "You will not understand what I'm going through until you lose someone you love, like Katherine."

He put his head down in shame. "Mom, I'm sorry," he said, when he realized how upset he'd made her.

Katherine's eyes darted from one to the other without saying a word. She looked as if she was about to cry seeing her husband and mother-in-law argue. She reached down and took a sip of her water with her hand shaking.

Though the dinner didn't go as well as Vivienne had planned, Brian hugged her before they left at the door.

"I'll e-mail you my itinerary," she said to him. "You'll think about taking over the house?"

He nodded. "Of course. I know that you and Dad planned that we would take it over someday. I just didn't expect to do it so soon."

"Well, does it really make sense for me to stay here in such a large empty house? I'd prefer to have something much smaller and easier to care for near the studio."

"Well please don't make any decisions about that until I can help you. We can go look at a few properties together if you'd like. I know a few reputable real-estate agents."

She smiled. "They would probably say they know a few 'reputable lawyers.'"

He smiled.

She looped her arm in his as they walked to the door. "That would be nice. Thank you."

He hugged her again. "I love you, Mom," he whispered in her ear. "I'm really sorry."

"Brian, it's all right. You felt an obligation to care for me the way your father did, but that's not going to work. I have to live my life the way *I* need to, not the way your father wanted me to. Thank you for understanding."

She hugged Katherine, who couldn't contain her emotions any longer. Tears streamed down her face as she watched the two of them. "Everything's fine. You two get home before it gets too late now."

"Can I drive you to the airport?" Brian asked.

"Of course, but you don't need to. I can take a cab."

"I want to, Mom."

"OK, I'll see you then." And she waved as they walked out away from the ambient light of the porch and into the dark toward their car. As their headlights descended, she wished them a safe trip home. She never took for granted a loved one leaving since Todd's death. So thankful she was that she and her son came to an agreed truce before they left that she too cried as they departed.

Knowing it wouldn't be an easy task to convince Brian she was taking more control over her own life, she felt a little guilty, but he had to learn that she also had a will in her own life.

She walked back inside the house after they were gone and unlike times past, she locked her own door and set the alarm on her own time.

❦ 25 ❦

October 20, 1989
Washington Mutual Building
Seattle Washington

TODD SAT AT HIS DESK HAVING HAD LITTLE SLEEP THE NIGHT before since the new baby now suffered from colic. He found it amazing how someone so little could cry so much and cause two grown adults so much sleep deprivation. It was almost a relief to leave the house, not because he didn't love his family but because his nerves would rattle less than they would even facing a court day at its worst. There was something about the cry of one of his own children that kept him on the edge of losing his mind. He couldn't fathom how Vivienne handled the stress so well. She was a remarkably patient mother. No matter how intense the crying or loss of sleep, she would still look at him with a contented smile despite the chaos. As if she were saying, "This is the life!" She was entirely happy that these two beings had completely disrupted their blissful existence.

"Good morning, Mr. Mathis," his assistant said as she came

137

through his office door like every morning. She was a strong, stout woman in her fifties. He suspected a Norwegian background, which was common in the area, but he'd never asked. She still wore an elaborate beehive hairdo in gray tones, a style from decades past, and he imagined the intricate style must take a lot of time to do every morning. She was a fearsome character and would make anyone a wonderful grandmother. Charlie had once referred to her as Mother Goose, and Todd dared him to say it to her face. Charlie declined immediately. Todd was certain she kept a rolling pin underneath her desk. No one messed with her, and that's why he hired her in the first place. Of all the attractive and capable assistants sent to him by the hiring service to interview, they were surprised that Todd requested her and even asked him why. He'd said she was the most capable and left it at that, daring them to mention her lack of attractiveness, which seemed to be what most lawyers went for.

Though this time she looked at him with a bit of concern for his rumpled appearance. He was dressed as usual, but his hair was sticking up in odd places. He'd been up half the night with the baby since Izzy was sick with a cold and Vivienne was caring for her. He'd showered like any typical day, but for some reason his hair just wouldn't comb down straight. "You, uh, look a bit exhausted."

He nodded in agreement and smiled like a maniac. "Yeah, and I have court in an hour too."

"The baby's keeping you up." It wasn't a question. She more or less just stated the fact as is. "I'll get you some coffee. Have you eaten anything?" She pointed at his shirt. "Oh, and you have a spot there."

Todd looked down below his right clavicle and sure enough, a round yellowish blob of goo showcased itself. He shook his head in disbelief.

"It's all right," she said in a soothing tone. "That's why we keep a backup set." She retreated, and he heard her fumbling around in the office closet. She returned just as quickly with another shirt, still enclosed in the dry cleaner's plastic sheeting.

"Ah, thank you." He stood and retrieved the shirt from her while she dropped off the bundle of daily mail.

"You change into that, and I'll go and get you some strong coffee and a toasted bagel. Here's the mail too. Sound good?"

"Yes, thank you so much."

As she closed the door, he undressed and quickly changed his shirt, replacing the tie he'd worn that morning as well. Then he sat back down and pushed the mail aside to go over his brief before his court appearance in an hour, though he noticed a thick envelope with something bulky inside. He typically only received envelopes with reams of paper through the mail, not actual packages, and he had no idea what might be inside. Perhaps a late gift for the baby? He flipped the padded envelope over and noticed the address was on a typed label. His heart began to beat a little faster. He opened the envelope. There was no paper inside. He turned the envelope over and dumped the contents out onto his desk, and the sight of the object startled him so much he shoved his chair away from the desk as if it were a snake or something as equally venomous.

Todd grabbed the phone and called home immediately, brushing the sweat from his brow. "Come on, Vivienne; pick up. *Please* pick up."

"Hello?" Vivienne answered with Brian crying in the background.

"Hi, honey. Everything OK?"

"Yes, of course. Don't you have court soon?"

"Yeah, I just..." *She'll think I'm nuts, and she's already got too much to deal with.* "I just wanted to hear your voice. Sorry things are so hard lately."

"I'm fine, Todd. Are you OK? Is there something wrong?"

"No. No, just thinking of you. I'll try to be home as soon as I can so you can catch a nap. I love you."

"I love you too, honey. I'll see you when you get home. Good luck in court."

"Thanks, Vivienne. Can you please make sure the doors are locked? I think I forgot."

Her voice sounded a little suspicious. "All right. I'll make sure. Don't worry about us, Todd. We're fine."

"Oh, I know. Just please make sure, or it will bug me all day."

"OK, if it will make you feel better."

"It will, thank you. See you later."

He hung up the phone, carefully laying the receiver into the cradle. *What does this mean?*

He stared down at the tortoiseshell hair clip, the one that Vivienne's grandmother had given her long ago. *Hadn't Vivienne mentioned losing it?* He'd know that clip anywhere. He'd taken it off of Vivienne countless times, watching how her hair cascade down to her shoulders. She wore it often. He'd learned to undo the clasp with just one hand, a feat he was proud of.

He flipped through his Rolodex, selected a card and then picked up the phone again after checking the time. He dialed a number while he put the clip back into the envelope from which it came. That's when his secretary returned with his coffee and the bagel.

He waved her in, and she sat the plate down on his desk. She gave him a questioning look and then left the office, closing the door behind her. "Yes, Detective Glenn, please. Can I leave a message? Please tell him I need to speak with him after, say, two this afternoon. I'll be in court until then. Yes, Todd Mathis. That's right. Thank you." He'd ended the call. A thought then occurred to him that maybe Vivienne had lost the clip and someone was just trying to return it to her. Perhaps at the doctor's office. He flipped the envelope over again. There was no return address, just like the threatening letter sent to the house.

The alternative was too scary to think about. She usually kept the clip on the top of their dresser when she wasn't wearing it, next to her hairbrush. *God, someone's been in my home...*

The secretary opened the door. "Mr. Mathis, you need to get to court. You haven't touched your breakfast. Are you feeling OK? You're white as a sheet."

He barely heard her words and then snapped out of it. "Yeah, I'm all right." He grabbed his briefcase, stuffed the envelope with the clip inside, and then picked up his coffee and headed for the door. "Can you clear any appointments I have this afternoon? I've got something I have to do."

"Of, course. It's Friday anyway. You should go home and get some rest," she said, with an encouraging smile.

"Thanks, I might do that." He left the office and had a scheduled cab waiting for him to drive the few blocks it took to get to the King County Courthouse. All the while, he could think of nothing but the possibility that someone had been in his home and wished to do him and his family harm. But who? Who would want to do this? As Charlie said, there were many wackos out there, and in their line of business, one makes enemies. He wasn't naïve about the risks, but what was he going to do about it? The police were little help. He couldn't really blame them. There wasn't a lot to go on. And he knew the first argument over the hair clip would be that some Good Samaritan had found it, knowing its owner, and just mailed it to his office instead of their home since that address wasn't readily available. But it wasn't a Good Samaritan. His gut told him so. No, this was the same guy who sent the threatening letter. He was sure of it.

❧ 26 ❧

P resent
Lake Union, Washington

VIVIENNE CHECKED HER LIST FOR THE MILLIONTH TIME AND left the last of the auction packages by her front door for the mailman to retrieve at his regular time.

Brian's tires crunched along the gravel. When she looked out the window, she saw that he'd brought Katherine's car instead of his sports car, which was nice because there was more room for the luggage and she hated sitting so low to the ground in Seattle traffic. It made her feel vulnerable next to the large trucks.

The sun was dim yet at only five in the morning. A light layer of moisture covered everything, and when she opened the front door, she felt the wet mist against her face. Brian had left the car running but got out and ran up to the door.

"I'll help you with those, Mom." He reached for her luggage. "Is this all you're taking? What about those packages?"

Vivienne smiled. "Those are for the mailman to pick up. We'll leave those there. I don't need that much really. I have several pieces that will intermix to make different outfits. I packed another collapsible bag for the items I'm sure I'll return with as well."

"That's a good idea."

He brought her suitcases to the trunk of the car, and she slid into the passenger seat. When he sat behind the wheel, he looked as tired as a delivery doctor. "You didn't have to get up so early, Brian."

"I wanted to, Mom. Let me do this, please."

"Thank you," she said, and he backed out of the driveway.

On their way to the airport, she asked if he and Katherine had made any decisions about the house. "Yes, we thought about the offer and decided you're probably right. Sybil is just starting school next year, and it's undoubtedly better we get her settled in before she does. Katherine wants her to go the academy where I went and the drive from here isn't nearly as far as from our current place.

"And Katherine's OK with moving into your childhood home?"

He smiled at her. "I think if this were a regular childhood home, there might be a problem, but to live on Lake Union... that's a treasure. So no, she's totally open to the idea."

"Oh, good. I don't want there to be any problems."

He reached for her hand as he drove. "Mom, I hope we're OK. I just don't want you to suffer. I know now that you're trying to do what you need to do to survive without Dad. I'm sorry I didn't see that before."

She squeezed his hand back. "It's OK, Brian. You're a good son. Your father was very proud of you. There's nothing wrong with trying to protect your family, but you have to let them live too. That's not something your father understood very well. He had his own reasons for protecting me the way he did. It wasn't always right, but I let him do it, though it wasn't healthy. I could have resisted the overprotection, but that security gave him a peace of mind that he needed. Now he's gone. And I have to live again. I'll let you take over when I'm drooling on myself. Deal?"

He huffed, not expecting a bit of humor from his mother over this solemn conversation. "Agreed."

Once at SeaTac Airport, he parked in the metered area and walked with his mom to check in her bags for her flight. He made sure she had everything she needed. Vivienne could tell he was still apprehensive about the trip she was about to take on her own.

"Don't worry. Izzy's on the other side, and I'm going to be fine."

He held her at arm's length, looking very concerned. "Did you charge your cell phone?"

She smiled, "Yes, of course."

"Don't talk to these people sitting next to you, Mom. There are a lot of con artists that prey on people your age in airports."

"I'm sure that's true." She decided not to take offense to the "your age" comment.

"And try to stay out of the bathrooms."

"OK, I won't drink anything." She could tell he was kind of, sort of kidding.

He hugged her close. "Please text me when you get to your first stop."

"Brian, I'm going to be fine. Wait until Sybil leaves for summer camp."

"Are you kidding? She's not going to summer camp. Those places are loaded with lice and Legionaries disease."

Vivienne laughed. "Oh, Brian." She shook her head.

He smiled. "Well, you'd better go," he said, and prodded her on to the security line. She kissed him one last time. He looked so worried about her. She queued up in the line. "Go ahead and go. I'll text you from the gate, I promise."

"*Please*, have a safe trip," he said, and his eyes looked utterly terrified to her. It was the first time she realized that her son was afraid not of her lack of protection but of losing her too. He'd lost his father to a careless accident and perhaps she hadn't realized how much his father's death had affected her son.

"Brian, I promise you, I will be fine."

He smiled again. His face was red with emotion, and he blinked back tears. He turned and waved once more before he was gone.

More people joined in the security line behind her, already showing their frustration with body language, as she watched her son's back walk down the corridor, his posture hunched and burdened.

She flipped out her phone once she'd successfully cleared security and got to the first gate of many. She smiled and took a selfie and sent the picture to Brian. "Made it to my first gate of many." She'd decided to make the trip as positive as possible and to chronicle the adventure with pictures to include her son in on her many travels, hoping that this way he would see she needed this freedom and that it was a good thing she was finally spreading her wings.

❧ 27 ❧

O
ctober 29, 1989
     Seattle Police Station
     Seattle, Washington

TODD WAITED PATIENTLY FOR THE DETECTIVE TO SEE HIM. HIS
court appearance had gone badly. Not because he didn't win the
motion to dismiss the case but because he was so utterly
distracted that eventually the judge admonished him in front of
the court. He couldn't blame the man. He *was* distracted.
Distracted in the worst of ways: out of fear for his family, so much
so that he found himself flashing back to old memories. Those of
his father's hand raised above his mother's fearful face, and her
cries late at night.

He sat in a textured vinyl beige chair in the small waiting
room of the police station among a group of what Todd could
only surmise were ladies of the night. Either that or they were
there to bail someone out. He wasn't sure. He leaned his head
against the wall, so dirty from others' similar positions that he
jerked away after realizing he was probably smearing other

people's hair oil into his own. The lady next to him was smacking her gum in a way that was like accidently scratching a fork against china over and over again, driving him crazy, except that she was doing it on purpose, knowing full well the effect she was having on him by the sneering smile she wore. Her red lipstick was at least five shades too bright for this time of day and, against her pale skin, reminded him of a sadistic vampire.

Todd was so aggravated by then that he was about to say something like, "Can you please knock that off?" when the bald officer at the desk said, "Mr. Mathis, Detective Glenn can see you now."

An hour later, Todd was even more frustrated. "Look, I know this guy is threatening my family. Vivienne didn't drop the clip in the grocery store or at the doctor's office or even at the mall, like you suggest. These envelopes are the same." Todd knew he was losing his cool, but there was nothing he could do about it. "This asshole was in my *goddam house!*"

At some point in his tirade, he had stood, yelling at the detective, and he knew that was not a productive thing to do, not in a police station. A younger officer was also standing nearby, with his hand over his weapon, and he looked ready to use it. Though Detective Glenn waved the officer down.

"Mr. Mathis, please calm down."

Todd looked around the station, and he'd apparently gotten all their attention from the concerned stares pointed in his direction. He sat down in the chair again next to the detective's desk. The detective began typing on his typewriter again, taking his statement.

Todd looked around the room, the younger officer still tossing concerned glances in his direction.

Detective Glenn finally turned to him. "Have any of your past clients verbally threatened you in any way?"

"No." Todd shook his head. He'd certainly had clients unhappy with their outcome, but none of them had held him as the ultimate person responsible for their actions. Most people were reasonable.

"You don't have any idea who this person could be?"

"I really don't. If I did, we would be having a very different conversation altogether."

Detective Glen looked at him with admonishment. He was at least a decade older than Todd, and he used that fatherly brow when he said, "Mr. Mathis, I don't recommend you engage anyone. If there is a clear threat, call us. We'll handle it. Unfortunately, there just isn't enough to go on here. There was no other note with the hair clip. You haven't noticed any signs of forced entry into your home. It could be...I mean *could be*...someone returning a lost item. So they forgot to put in a note. Or they just wanted to do it anonymously. The first threatening letter, sure. But we have no idea who could have done this, as you said yourself, and...you are a lawyer. You're going to have threats, Mr. Mathis."

Did they think he didn't know that? That perhaps he was overreacting? Todd took in a deep breath. He wanted to strangle the detective. That's all there was to it. The man wasn't going to do his job. He set his jaw and nodded his head and rubbed his face. *What can I do to keep her safe then?* That was the only thing he could think of. These people don't even believe me.

He'd suddenly made up his mind. He'd had an idea, and it was the only thing he could think to do.

❄ 28 ❄

P resent
   Paris, France

AFTER ONLY A FEW HOURS' SLEEP, ISABEL WOKE TO HER PHONE
vibrating on her nightstand. She typically let the phone go into
sleep mode except for her brother's and her mother's numbers.
Those were let through no matter the hour. When she looked at
the number and the hour, she was beginning to regret that
decision.

"Izzy, has Mom's flight arrived yet?"

"Brian, it's two in the morning, and I had at least another hour
to sleep before I had to get up. Her flight isn't scheduled to arrive
for a couple of hours. What's the matter with you? You sound
worried. Did something happen?"

"I am worried. I haven't heard from her since she left the
stopover in Frankfort. Have you?"

Her brother, even as a little boy, needed extra reassurances.
"No, it was late, Brian. She's probably tired and didn't want to

bother us either. I'll have her contact you as soon as I see her, OK? Brian, are you all right, really?" She had to ask because he didn't sound like himself, and she was beginning to worry more about her little brother. She knew he was having a hard time with their mother's new lifestyle changes, but she never expected him to take it like this. Maybe he took their father's death harder than she thought.

His voice came through exhausted. She wondered if he'd slept at all since their mother had left the states. "Yeah...yeah, I'm fine. She's just making a lot of new decisions, and it has me worried about her."

In a soothing tone, Isabel said, "I would have thought that her coming here might make you relax a little. Especially since you suspect Dad was trying to tell you that she was in danger of some kind. She's out of danger here, Brian. It's OK for her to visit me. It's a normal thing to do for a mom."

"It's not that. She's working again too. She sold a lot of the stuff in the house, and she doesn't want to live there anymore. Katherine and I are going to take it over. Did you even know about that?"

"No, but that's her choice. It's an awfully big house for one person. I can see why she'd want something smaller. She practically spends her days cleaning it as it is. She misses Dad terribly, Brian. Imagine having to live there by yourself with all their memories stored in that place. I'm afraid it would drive me insane. Have you heard anything else about the investigation?"

"No, nothing. Yeah, you're probably right. Still, I hope she doesn't regret the decisions in time."

She glanced at the time on her watch. "OK, well I guess I can get ready. At least now I can have more than one cup of coffee before going there to fetch her from the airport. I'll have her contact you as soon as I see her, so don't worry, Brian. And please, try to get some sleep."

"I will, bye, Sis," Brian said, and hung up. Though she doubted his few words.

Isabel put the phone down and quickly gathered her things to shower. After she had a bite to eat and a second cup of coffee, she had just enough time to go and retrieve her mother. She expected her mom to be exhausted from the long trip, and when they returned to Isabel's flat, the thought of taking a nap would be the first order of business.

Elated that her mother had finally taken her offer to come and visit, she quickly brushed out her long dark hair and put it up in a ponytail and then grabbed her cross-body purse. She'd called for a taxi the night before, and when she looked out the window down to the street below lined with a few light poles illuminating the early-morning hour, she saw a regular car with the assigned plaque on the side of the door indicating that he was an official taxi service. It wasn't worth risking one of the fly-by-night unofficial taxi offers so prevalent now in Paris, not with her mother in tow.

A friend of hers had recently tried one and ended with the journey much lighter than just the fare intended. That was enough of a warning for her to never try the ones without the official plaque. She chalked the incident up as a learning experience she'd never wager against. Even the Uber concept from the United States was under fire in France. Most citizens just found taking unofficial taxis not worth the risk of theft or worse.

Isabel rode through the streets of Paris wondering about what her mother would think of the "city of light" as she stared out the window. Early fall in Paris was a lovely time to visit. Much less crowded than in the summer months, the Palais-Royal Gardens were beautiful that time of year, with the added bonus of autumn's hues.

Isabel flashed on a memory of her mother sketching from a park bench in the Seattle Japanese Gardens while she and her brother ran around and chased the ducks or saw who could find the most winged maple seed pods floating gracefully on the wind before they fell like feathers to the ground. That memory was when she and her brother were only preschool aged. It seemed they went to the parks less and less as they aged. Isabel wasn't sure if that was because of her father's overprotectiveness or simply the way life progresses from childhood. One thing was for certain: her mother loved time spent outdoors, and she did it less and less, visiting places she loved as time went on.

As her taxi raced through the streets, she clenched the seat when one of many scooters zipped in front of her driver, causing the driver to break quickly. "*Enfoiré, regarde où tu vas!*" yelled the driver, and used hand gestures to get his point across.

She paid little attention to the irate exchange. Driving in Paris was a contact sport for most. Luckily, she and her mother would walk to the many places she wanted her to see or take the train, which was usually pretty safe.

On one occasion she'd hoped they would visit Versailles, which was best viewed in the autumn months, with the many gardens in full bloom. The last time Isabel had visited, she couldn't help but feel guilty that her mother wasn't with her, knowing how much she would enjoy the grand palace.

Before she knew it, the taxi stopped at the airport. He said, "Voilà, *vous y êtes.*"

"*Combien vous dois-je?*" She asked how much the fare was.

"*Cinquante euros, s'il vous plaît,*" he said.

She handed him the money, and as she departed she began to say, "Merci," though he'd already zoomed away before her feet had barely hit the pavement and she finished the greeting, leaving her to stand there in the damp street alone. Which was how taxi drivers were in France. Always in a rush for the next fare that it seemed like a game quest that they were always on the losing end of.

Isabel had just walked into the airport when her phone buzzed with a text message.

"I'm here," it read.

Isabel hazily looked at the reader board for arriving flights and rushed over to the right arrival terminal near the baggage claim. There were throngs of sleepy individuals standing and waiting for someone to arrive without saying much, only a pall of quiet anticipation. When several new arrivals began walking their way, the quiet crowd grew a little restless and then a few jockeyed for position to see if they recognized those they were waiting for. Isabel too stepped from right to left on to her tiptoes to look at the crowd coming in, vying to see her mother among the strangers arriving. Soon, the quiet atmosphere from before erupted in conversation as loved ones found their matches.

Isabel couldn't help but to move forward through the throngs as those who'd found their person slipped behind the rest and nearer to the baggage claim. Then Isabel sighted a slight woman coming her way, and for a split second, she didn't recognize the beaming smile. He mother had lost weight, and it was noticeable.

"Mother!" Isabel yelled. She hadn't expected the strong emotion springing from herself.

Vivienne rushed into her daughter's open arms. "Isabel," she said, and stroked her daughter's hair.

"I can't believe you're here. I'm so happy you made it," she said to her mother. She looked a little tired, but despite that, she was cheerful.

"Me too. I can't believe it myself."

"Are you exhausted?"

She nodded. "I am a little, but what a wonderful trip."

"Oh, I hate it now. I'm so over international travel. I was so excited when I was younger getting to fly overseas. Now, it's the biggest drag ever." She laughed.

"I had no problems. I was a little late getting to the gate in Frankfurt, but other than that, no issues at all."

"Oh, please text Brian right away. He's about to have a coronary."

"Oh my. Wait until Sybil gets older. He's in for a lot of late nights," she said as she sent a text to Brian. "I'll call him too, when we get to your place, to let him know I made it in one piece."

"I'm sure if there was a way to stunt Sybil's growth, he'd do it." Isabel laughed.

"Keep that to yourself. Don't give him any ideas. I don't blame him, really. Let's pick up my luggage."

"I think when we get back to the flat, you should try to sleep for a couple of hours after you call Brian, and then we'll go out for brunch. How does that sound?"

"Perfect," Vivienne said, and slipped her arm through her daughter's as they made their way to pick up her luggage.

❦ 29 ❦

P ast
Seattle, Washington

TODD RETURNED HOME LATER THAT EVENING. LONG AFTER HIS
usual time. When he'd turned the knob on the door, it was open
and not locked. His heart pounded as he stepped over the threshold. "Vivienne?" There was no answer. He took a few steps inside
the foyer. "Vivienne?" he yelled again. *Oh my God. I'm too late!* A
few more seconds passed as he waited, expecting the worst, and
listened. Only the drip, drip of the kitchen faucet, reminding him
it needed tightening, could be heard. "Viv...?"

"We're out here, darling," she called from the backyard
beyond the living room. He then noticed the screen door was half
open. *Oh, thank God!* he cried within.

He locked and bolted the front door and dropped his keys and
briefcase in the hall. When he stepped on the mat at the back
door, he found Vivienne holding baby Brian and sitting on the
edge of the sandbox he'd built for Isabel, while Izzy was happily

dumping cups of sand one after the other and running her tiny fingers through the mounds.

When his little girl noticed him standing in the doorway beyond her mother, she stood up and splayed her arms wide, tossing sand everywhere, and greeted him. "Daddy's home!" He'd never tire of coming home to such bliss.

He rolled up his sleeves, intent on helping Izzy, when he said, "You left the front door unlocked, Viv. Anyone could have walked right inside, and you'd never know about it until it was too late. You can't do that." He was nauseated at the thought of what might have happened.

"Oh, I'm sorry," she said. "I brought in groceries, and I must have forgotten."

He bent down and kissed her. "Please don't forget again. It makes me worry about you here by yourself."

He was shaking, and he hoped she hadn't noticed.

"Are you hungry? I saved dinner for you."

"Not right away," he said, and dove his hands into the sand with Izzy.

Later, after the sandbox and bath time, a layer of sand covered the bottom of the tub. When Isabel was through with her bath, she ran down the hallway dressed in a fresh nightgown and with damp hair, Todd chased her and wrangled her into bed. There were stories and a good-night kiss and lights went off. He barely closed the door so that a sliver of light cascaded inside, just so he could peer in to see if she was safe in bed.

Vivienne was doing the dishes after having put down baby Brian as well. He walked past. "I have to get something from the car. I'll be right back," he said, and when he returned he had a brown paper bag from the hardware store.

When she saw it, she said, "What are you doing?"

He acted nonchalant. "Oh, I noticed this doorknob sticking the other day and meant to pick up a new dead bolt. I just got around to it on the way home. It'll just take me a second to install it.

"Oh, I never noticed a problem with it sticking."

"Well, you do have your hands full all day. You probably just never noticed. I don't want it to jam on you and have you and children locked out one day," he said. He knelt down and replaced the deadbolt, hoping she didn't ask any more questions. After the installation, she put the new keys on her keyring and his. Mentally, he was thinking changing the locks was one tiny layer of protection. There was no other way into this house, and no visible signs of how the guy broke in.

Later that evening they were both in bed, Vivienne reading a little of her current novel as he watched the news. He raised the remote and hit the power button when he'd had enough and when he decided on the best way to broach the next subject with Vivienne.

"Hey, I got a call today from an old friend. He told me that a piece of property was about to hit the market on Lake Union. I've always wanted to live there. Why don't we go and see the house this weekend?"

She put her book down on the nightstand, dog-earing the page she was on, and looked a little surprised by the news. "But I thought you liked living here."

"I do, but if this property is everything he says it is, we can't pass it up. Those lots only come open every few generations. We could pass it down to the kids when we retire."

He watched for her reaction. Her light-blue eyes looked pensive. For anything in the world, he didn't want her to worry. His goal in life was to love and protect her. Those were his vows, and he'd taken them seriously when he committed to her.

She thought about what it would be like to move there for a minute. "I'm perfectly happy here, Todd, but if that's what you want to do. I'd rather make a move before Izzy is preschool age."

He ran the back of his hand down her cheek. He'd do anything to keep her safe, and moving her was the only thing he could think of. Hell, he'd relocate her across the state if he thought that was an option, but for now, he could only move her across the city. He'd have their address unpublished. He'd find a way to keep the threat away from her. He didn't want her ever concerned by this. She had enough to do all day taking care of the children, and he didn't want to ruin that perfect world for her. It was his job to protect her from all the evils of the world, and he would do so until his last dying breath.

❧ 30 ❧

P**resent**
Paris, France

IN THE FIRST WEEK, ISABEL PLAYED TOUR GUIDE AND BROUGHT Vivienne to all the local attractions, and Vivienne was just starting to get into the relaxed rhythm of the local people.

"How do the French stay so fit?" Vivienne asked her daughter as they sat in an outdoor café enjoying espresso with the slightly breezy weather, and the most delicious buttery croissant she'd ever tasted. The flaky croissant was the most decadent treat, incomparable to the many versions in the United States. She'd never dreamed they could be so good. They watched all the people coming and going in the park connected to the café.

"First of all," Isabel began, "they walk everywhere." She raised her hand as if to say, *As you can see*. "And they don't exercise the way Americans do. They think that's a waste of one's energy, and secondly...they don't *eat* the croissants." She ended with a smile.

Vivienne laughed. "I'm afraid I would be huge because I *would* eat the croissants every day. They're so good."

"I must admit, when I first came, I put on a few pounds despite all the walking. The food is so good here. Then, I started refraining a little and rewarding myself by the end of the week. It's a balance. Food is thought of differently here. It's meant to be savored, not just to sustain. It's common to have a three-hour meal at a restaurant until late in the evening. You're supposed to linger and enjoy life's little nuances."

"Seems better than how Americans eat."

"I don't think it's better. It's just different than the way Americans look at things. Americans are always trying to streamline things to make them more logical, more advanced, and more time efficient. The French attitude is much different. It's more like stop and smell the roses. Appreciate everything around you. One is not a better approach to life. They are both applicable to different situations."

Vivienne was at that moment so proud of her daughter. Her insight into the area was a tribute to the person she had raised. "You're amazing." She laughed. "I could not love you more. Look who you have become."

"Oh, Mom!" Izzy said, and that statement made her mother laugh even harder with joy.

That's when Vivienne's phone vibrated. She had her purse on her lap and had not paid much attention to her phone since her arrival over a week ago, except to talk to reassure Brian occasionally. She'd taken several photos with her cell while she was there of course, but the last several hours she was doing nothing more than enjoying her daughter and her surroundings. She reached inside and saw there was a missed call from Brian. She texted him back. *Having lunch with Izzy. I'll call back later.*

He texted back immediately and said, *This is Katherine. Please call now. There's a problem.*

"Mom, what is it?" Isabel asked at her mother's stricken expression.

"It's Katherine. Something's happened," she said as she dialed. Vivienne couldn't imagine a scenario where Katherine would use Brian's phone unless there was some emergency. Suddenly, seeing Todd's mangled body flashed through her mind as he laid on the metal table, a blue paper sheet drawn over his remains.

"Katherine? What's going on?"

Her voice was hushed but panicked. "It's Brian. He's in the hospital having surgery. He's been shot."

All her breath suddenly escaped her body as her vision suddenly narrowed, with black pools surrounding her. Katherine was on the verge of hysteria. "Katherine, what happened?"

She was barely able to calm herself. "He was um...going to your house after the security company phoned us, saying there was a break-in last night. They'd sent the police to check it out last night, but they found nothing so Brian went early this morning before work to check on things. And when he was inside trying all the locks, someone else was there too and shot him. Brian was able to get up and ran out the door and got into his car and drove away before the shooter could get to him again. He drove himself straight to the hospital. Someone found him unconscious in the loading area."

As Katherine recounted the event, every hair on Vivienne stood alert. A dreadful chill took her over. "Oh my God." She stood in the middle of the café, trembling with fear. "What...what did the doctor say?"

Katherine took a moment to control her emotions before she answered. "He has, um, some internal injuries. They're doing exploratory surgery now and trying to see the extent of the damage. Vivienne, I'm so scared. He could die." She broke down crying then.

Vivienne took a deep breath as her daughter-in-law lost it on the phone. "Where are the children now, Katherine?"

"They're with my sister."

"OK, I'm catching the next flight home. I'm so sorry, Katherine. I'll be there as soon as I can. Call or text me with any updates. Will you?"

"I will," she said meekly and hung up.

Isabel, having heard every word, stared at her mother in disbelief. All color drained from her expression.

"Oh my God—Brian!"

❧ 3 1 ❧

O ctober 29, 1989
     Lake Union, Washington

VIVIENNE AND TODD WALKED THROUGH THE HOUSE ON LAKE Union. There was nothing like it anywhere else. A mansion on a lake that would likely never come up for sale again. How could they pass it up? They walked hand in hand down the dock, watching the sunset. The realtor clearly knew the best time to show them the house.

"Nothing can beat that sunset," Todd said.

"We'd love it here," Vivienne said. "What a great place for the kids to grow up."

He smiled at her. She kissed him. "Maybe at night, by the light of the moon, we could even skinny dip," he teased, and pulled her close.

"Not unless you want all our neighbors to see. We're not exactly hidden here."

"True," he thought, though they would be protected on paper.

He'd taken pains to make sure the address was hidden from public view and that their number was unlisted. That's all he could do for now until he knew where the threat was coming from.

He'd begun going through his clients one by one on his own. His secretary was curious, but he'd made an excuse that he was just looking for a justification from a past client to use for a new case, though he couldn't remember which one of his many past clients. So she brought the files to him in chronological order going back nearly till his very first case over ten years before.

For each file, he noted who was involved and researched where that person was, if he or she had a reasonable grudge against him, and whether the person could be the likely culprit. So far he had no one with an applicable motive to harass him and threaten the life of his wife, but he would keep looking a little each day despite that.

❧

ONE MONTH LATER, THEY MOVED INTO THE HOUSE ON LAKE Union. Neighbors welcomed them into the fold. They were mostly elderly and kept to themselves for the most part, though on occasion they'd receive an invitation to dinner.

Six months later, Todd sat in his law office when his friend, the real-estate agent, called. It seemed a house fire had engulfed his old house overnight. They expected an issue with faulty wiring since the husband had installed a new bedroom addition.

The father was able to get his children to safety but the wife had died of smoke inhalation. They'd tried to revive her on the front lawn. It was awful news, and the agent was just letting him know what had happened out of courtesy. He didn't want for him to hear it on the news.

Todd hung up the phone. Sat the receiver into the cradle carefully. Then he put his hand to his mouth and closed his eyes. His mind replaced Vivienne's image with that of the new owner's wife, a house in a blaze behind her body lying on the lawn. *It can't be. God, please don't let this be connected to the threat.*

In the end, it didn't matter. There was no proof a month later. The death of the wife was declared accidental. The cause was listed as they suspected: faulty wiring from the new addition. The mother had died in her bed. There was no evidence of foul play. No evidence of a break-in. Nothing to indicate the death was malicious in any way.

Still, Todd couldn't let the odd connection go. He was utterly terrified the mother's death was a hit and was meant for Vivienne. He didn't waste his time alerting Detective Glenn of his suspicions. If the police had not taken the reappearing hair clip as evidence, they certainly would not pay any heed to this death already explained as an unfortunate accident.

It was enough that when he'd reached home that day, Vivienne had a startled look as he came through the door. "Honey, one of the neighbors called and said our old house burned down last night. The wife died. I'm so horrified. How can something like that happen?" she'd said, choking out the last few words. He'd held her tight. She saw in his eyes that he'd already known. He told her the real-estate agent had phoned him that morning, and he was going to tell her about the accident when he came home.

She'd cried for this mother she'd never met. That same mother was sleeping in her room peacefully when her life had left her body, the same place Vivienne spent many nights sleeping next to Todd, feeling safe in his arms.

❦ 32 ❦

P resent
Paris, France

"I'M COMING," ISABEL SAID. "IT'S A FAMILY EMERGENCY. They'll understand." She'd already taken time off to show her mother around Paris anyway. Isabel made a quick call, and all was set. She began stuffing a few items into her bag, and then they were hailing a taxi; this time anyone who stopped would do, even a ride from a hack. They didn't care.

At the airport, Isabel spoke fluent French at a rapid-fire pace, sometimes yelling at the attendant over the flight times. Vivienne had never seen her daughter take such charge before. If the circumstances weren't so tragic, she'd show more pride in her daughter, but this wasn't the time.

All she could think about now was Brian fighting for his life at Harborview Hospital in Seattle, which was nearly a world away.

While waiting for their first flight out of Paris to Frankfurt, Katherine texted that Brian was out of surgery and in stable condition. Vivienne wanted to know so much more but was afraid to ask. He was critical before. Did stable mean he was out of the woods? Where was he shot exactly, and what were his chances at a full recovery? Would he ever be the same, and how the hell was someone in her home with a gun? She pushed every question she had to the side because nothing mattered now, nothing but Brian's survival and getting to him as fast as she possibly could from across the Atlantic.

Somehow, Isabel was able to get them on the next crowded flight. They weren't able to sit together, but it didn't matter. Vivienne was inside herself. She kept thinking of Todd and how he'd died, so swiftly taken from her. *Not again. Please not my son,* she begged to any god who would listen to her. *I'll do anything, anything in the world. Just please don't take my son from me.*

Somehow she'd fallen asleep on the next trans-Atlantic flight. She and Isabel were together on that one at least. They held hands but did nothing more than that and slept the entire time. When they landed in Washington, DC, they again sat apart, and it seemed the closer they came to Seattle the more paranoid Vivienne's thoughts became. *Could this have something to do with Todd's death?* It was an illogical question, she knew. But having something like this happen so close to their first tragedy made little sense to her. *How could this happen? The universe wasn't this cruel.*

❧ 33 ❧

P ast
Seattle, Washington

"HEY, TODD, NICE GOING," CHARLES SAID AS HE'D LEFT THE King County Courthouse. He'd smiled and placed his hand in his pocket and looked down.

"Thank you, but the jury can take credit for this one. My client really was innocent. Thankfully they saw the case our way."

"Sure, that's what they all say. You want to grab a drink?"

Todd looked at his watch. "No, sorry. I can just make Izzy's soccer practice if I leave now. Maybe next week?"

"Yeah, sure. No problem. Have a great weekend."

"You too, Charlie."

Todd drove straight through the drizzling rain to Izzy's school, where her soccer practice was taking place in the adjacent field. As he pulled up, he could already see a line of parents and their colorful umbrellas in a row. A stack of juice boxes waited nearby along with boxes of granola bars. He often thought whoever invented juice in a box with tiny attached straws and a cookie masqueraded as a health food were geniuses. They'd never had either of those treats, now called childhood staples, when he was a kid. Juice in a giant bottle was a treat then. It seemed anywhere you went these days with children Izzy's age, juice boxes weren't far behind. Heck, he remembered only having milk or water as choices, and not only did he survive but he also had fewer cavities.

Todd stepped out of his drenched car with his overcoat on and spotted Vivienne on the right of the lineup, holding their toddler in her arms. Once Brian saw his father though, he reached for him and leaned out of his mother's arms so much so that Todd hurried and grabbed him before he was able to wrangle away from his mother completely and hit the wet ground. "Whew, thank you," she said to him.

He smiled. "How you doing, buddy?"

"Raining," Ben said pointing above with a tiny finger. Where Izzy had been an easy toddler, Brian was not. He spent his days challenging his mother and his evenings torturing his sister. Chasing her around with a worm he found in the backyard or pulling her long, dark braids to hear her squall. Some childhood rites of passage never changed.

Todd didn't mind. He loved every minute of their childhood. All the bumps and challenges; it was every bit of a wonderful experience he was short-changed of as a child himself. He kissed Vivienne and huddled next to her under the umbrella as they watched their daughter, dark braids dripping with rainwater as she ran after the ball ahead of the pack. "Go, Izzy!" he yelled. She heard his voice, looked back, and shot him a quick smile.

When practice was over, they headed home in a caravan of two cars, one child in each. He'd taken Isabel with him since Vivienne had the car seat for Brian in hers. Rainwater poured off Isabel onto his leather seats but he didn't mind. He laid his overcoat down over her when she started shivering and turned up the heat. "How was school?" he said in the rearview mirror.

"It was OK. Got a hundred on my spelling test."

"That's great, baby."

She smiled back at him, those dark braids and sky-blue eyes, with a smattering of freckles across her nose. She was everything a father wanted in a daughter. Strong and tough but gentle and kind. Always open to a hug, but she didn't let the boys push her around. He was proud of that. Sometimes she pushed herself too hard though, and he made a point of letting her know he didn't expect perfection, just hard work.

"But you know, As and Bs are fine with me."

She lolled back, obviously tired. "I know, Dad, but I like getting As."

He smiled and then pulled up behind Vivienne in the driveway. They ran for the front door, and on the porch Isabel wrung water from her braids and took off her muddy soccer shoes, leaving them by the front door.

Inside, he smelled what he hoped was chili, and when he went into the kitchen and washed his hands, he'd found Vivienne scooping up large ladlefuls into bowls from the slow cooker. God, how he loved that woman who thought ahead. Isabel sat at the table ready for her meal, Brian in his high chair, spoon in his hand.

"Izzy, do you want cheese on yours?" Vivienne asked.

"Yes, please, and tortillas chips too."

"No sour cream?"

She made a yucky face and shook her head. "No, please."

Todd laughed.

"Sour cream is an acquired taste," he said. Vivienne handed Todd Isabel's bowl, and he brought it to her and then went back for Brian's. He began to make a third trip as a waiter, but Vivienne was already coming into the dining room with both of theirs with all the topping options, including sour cream and chopped green onions.

"I love chili day," Todd said.

"Thank you. I knew it was going to rain a lot today, and hot chili seemed like a good idea."

Isabel was too busy eating her first bowl, and once she was finished, she had seconds.

Later that night, he and Vivienne laid in bed. He was going over his brief for the next day, when he thought about Isabel. He took off his reading glasses and said, "Do you think Izzy's too hard on herself in school? She was very proud she aced the spelling test, but I remember last week she cried for missing one word."

Vivienne let out a breath. "She's just like you, Todd. I think we should just keep reminding her that she doesn't have to be perfect. It's OK to miss one every now and then."

"Yeah, that's the same impression I'm getting." It was a grim statement. He didn't want one of his negative attributes also burdening his daughter. He realized she came by perfectionism naturally, but it could make life difficult at times.

"Hey, have you seen Brian's bear?"

"The brown one with the red-and-white scarf that he calls Beard?"

"Yeah, I can't find it anywhere, and he's going nuts when I put him down to sleep without that guy. This afternoon, he barely had a nap because he didn't have him to cuddle."

"*That's* why he was so crabby earlier."

"Yeah, it's like wrestling a tiger, that boy..."

He reached over and kissed Vivienne as they both turned off their lights. "No, I haven't seen it. Maybe it's under the seat in your car. I'll look for it tomorrow. Good night," he said.

"Good night."

❊ 34 ❊

P resent
Seattle, Washington

WHEN ISABEL AND VIVIENNE ARRIVED IN SEATTLE IT WAS eleven at night. They were both exhausted, having slept very little on the three flights. "Can we even see him, if we arrive this late at night?"

"It depends on his condition. I'll text Katherine and ask her."

Instead of texting back, Katherine called Vivienne right away. "Hi, Viv, they made me leave the hospital room. When I left, he was in stable condition. He was still asleep when the nurses shooed me out. She said I could come back in the morning and that they would call me if there were any changes in his condition. She also said they expected him to be stable through the night."

"OK, we just got in, so I think we'll go to the house and…"

"Oh, you can't go there." Katherine said. "They've got tape up. It's a crime scene. You can come here, and I'll put you two in my room. My mom is staying to watch the girls now, and she's sleeping in the spare room."

"That's very kind of you, but it's late, Katherine. We'll get a hotel room tonight near Harborview Hospital."

"Are you sure?"

"Yes, of course. It would take us another half an hour to drive there anyway, and you need your sleep. It's nearly midnight, and I'm sure you're exhausted. We'll catch a cab and stay here overnight and see you at the hospital in the morning."

"OK, I'm so sorry this happened, Vivienne. You must have been having a wonderful time in Paris before my call."

"Oh, don't feel bad. There's always Paris. I'll go back someday, but I had to come home as quick as I could. Get some sleep. I love you, and I'll see you both in the morning." She hung up then and gave Izzy a tired look. "We need to find a hotel for tonight."

"OK, no problem," Izzy said, and began pressing buttons on her phone. She then called someone while Vivienne located their bags. They dragged themselves through SeaTac Airport to the front entrance and hailed a cab. When they were finally seated, Isabel blurted out in French where to take them and then caught herself, shaking her head. "I mean...The Crown Plaza near Harborview Medical Center, please."

The cab driver drove through the night. Lights sped by them as Vivienne watched an all-seeing-eye medallion swing back and forth from the cab driver's rearview mirror. He'd caught her looking at it once, and she looked away, out her window. Isabel had leaned her head against the passenger side door and was probably sound asleep. Vivienne felt like sleeping too, but all she could think about was her son lying in a hospital bed with a life-threatening injury caused by a stranger who was in her house. She thought of Todd and what he would do in this instance, but for some reason her mind strained more and more to the past and how she couldn't help but feel that it was all her fault. She should never have left Seattle to begin with when Brian was so against the trip from the start. Todd wouldn't have wanted her to go. It wasn't safe, and Brian had tried to tell her that.

❧ 35 ❧

P ast
Seattle, Washington

Todd had a sinking feeling. Anything that came up missing always created a sense of dread for him that lasted weeks or until that item finally turned up. But a week had gone by, and not only did Brian not forget about the missing bear but when his assistant brought in a new bulky envelope with the daily mail, a familiar package sat on his desk in front of him like a harbinger of the hell he knew he'd be in if what he found inside was what he suspected.

With nearly a few months gone by without another threat, he'd hoped that his own personal bully was dead or reformed or he'd shaken him loose with the move they'd made to Lake Union.

He flipped the suede-colored package over. A typed address label and no return address. Postmarked from Seattle, same as before.

"Please don't let it be," he said. His office door was closed.

He'd pressed the package and tried to talk himself out of the fact that his young son's bear was inside. What would he do? What could he do?

"This can't be happening!" he said, and ripped the paper package open on one side. He dumped out the contents and had to shake the envelope a little. Out came the bear, slowly at first as the fur hugged the inside paper but came tumbling out with gravitational force. No note was inside, same as the hair clip years earlier.

The clip he'd given back to Vivienne, he'd said he'd found it in the grass in the backyard. It was a reasonable excuse, and she loved it as a family heirloom. Still, every time she wore the clip, the reminder killed him, made him wary of everything. He vowed he'd never do that again. He'd never return an object that was touched by whoever was doing this. At times, he was paranoid. This bear, he just couldn't. Someone had been in his house again and taken his son's toy. Fury ran through him. He swiped the contents off his desk with one arm. A desk lamp crashed to the floor along with the package, and the bear went flying across the office.

His assistant came running after hearing the glass from his lamp shatter against the floor. "Sir?"

Todd stood with his hands over his face. He walked over to the floor-to-ceiling windows of his office. "Leave it. I'll clean it up myself."

She closed the door quietly.

What the hell am I going to do?

He'd become too complacent and vowed to never let that happen again. Todd righted the items on his desk and cleaned up the mess he'd made. He called Detective Glenn and filed a police report this time not that it would do any good. Then he called a home security company.

Todd took the next week off. He explained to Vivienne that there had been several break-ins as of late in the surrounding neighborhood, and he was taking extra precautions. She'd protested as the cameras were installed and the strangers walked through their home with suggestions. She didn't want their house to seem like a prison, and she worried that the tactics he was employing were too invasive.

He made an excuse that another lawyer's family had been threatened, and he didn't want that to happen to them. "Vivienne, society, in general, is only one missed medication away from mass murder at any given moment. I'm a high-profile attorney. My *name* is everywhere. It's not hard to find out where I live, and there are people out there who would like to do me harm. The only thing they would have to do is act on impulse and hurt one of my family members. *No,* this isn't too much to ask to keep you safe."

She stood there stunned as he walked away. Strangers passed her in the hallway of her home. He'd visibly shook when he had to explain his feelings, and he worried his "tell" was more than his words conveyed.

Vivienne never protested again. He knew he'd scared her, but she was taking extra precautions now and that was the goal. She never forgot to lock the doors and set the alarm again. When he came home, everything was as it should be, with his family safe inside.

❧ 36 ❧

P resent
Seattle, Washington

VIVIENNE STARED DOWN AT HER SON AS HE LAY HELPLESS ON the hospital bed. The monitors beeped. Tubes were taped at the side of his mouth and his arms. Another drainage tube protruded from the side of his chest and led down to a container at the side of the bed. The nurses came in the room and watched the color of the contents seeping out of her son's body. They'd taken his pulse, flashed a light inside his eyes and smiled at her as she looked to them with questions left unanswered.

"The doctor is coming in soon," they would say. "He'll answer your questions then, Mrs. Mathis." Of course they knew she had questions. The nursing staff dealt with tragedies like this on a daily basis. What was routine for them was a nightmare to her. She couldn't imagine being a nurse and seeing that stricken look on a mother's face over and over again.

Katherine was there before they arrived. She was thin and frail and void of any color. This young woman was facing the possibility of her husband's death and that alone broke her heart, to see her daughter-in-law face something so dire, and she wasn't even there when it happened. She had to give her credit though; she was tough, and she handled the whole thing on her own and well at that. Vivienne wouldn't have handled the situation any better. Even so, a weight was visibly lifted off her shoulders when they arrived.

"How are the girls?"

"They're fine. My mom and sister are staying with them now. My dad and brother were here yesterday with me, but I'm so glad you're here now."

She'd broken down then, and Vivienne said, "I'm so sorry you had to face this on your own."

She shook her head. "My family was here. Dad spoke to the detective yesterday. Oh, the detective wanted you to call him this morning." Vivienne nodded as Katherine handed her a card from a Detective Glenn.

Isabel immediately took a hold of the card. "I'll call him now, Mom," she said, and disappeared from the room.

There was a rage growing in her daughter; she'd seen the same expression in her husband. Those two were just the same, and she feared what that might mean. She couldn't let Isabel take this on herself. It was too much to bear.

"I'll be right back, Katherine. Excuse me a second."

Katherine nodded but never took her eyes off her husband.

She too looked Brian over to assure herself of why she was concerned and left the room. Isabel was down the hall with her phone to one ear and her other hand waving up and down in frustration. Whoever was on the other end of that phone was getting an earful.

Vivienne came and stood in front of her with a look of admonishment. As if to say, "That isn't the way to handle things."

She cut her eyes from her mother and back to the void to her left. "Yes, Officer. No, we cannot go down there. But *you* can come here since we will not leave my brother's side until he is out of woods. You can speak to my mother then. Harborview, yes. That's fine. See you then."

She ended the call. "Mother, what do you expect? If you don't light a fire under them, they'll do the minimal."

Vivienne didn't argue. "They're coming here?"

"Yes, around noon they're coming to ask you a few questions and to take a statement."

"Do they have any answers yet? Fingerprints?"

"They wouldn't say over the phone. I think they know something though."

It was the not knowing that bothered her. Why would someone do this? Break into her home and then shoot her son the next day? Had the shooter waited there for him? She'd convinced herself it was a random break-in. The security people should have done a more thorough search. They had inspected the alert but only did a drive by, they said. As if a burglar would announce himself. They thought it was just a false alarm.

Then the next day, her son went to the house to make sure it was OK, and the perpetrator was still inside, gunning down her son when he arrived. It was as if the shooter waited inside intentionally for the right opportunity or the right person. *But why?*

❦ 37 ❦

Past
Fred's
Seattle, Washington

"CHARLIE, THE GUY WAS IN MY HOUSE *AGAIN*," TODD SAID, AND took another swig of his bourbon. Lights were dim at the bar, but Charlie saw his stricken expression well enough.

"You don't know that exactly. He might have picked the bear up from the kid covertly at the grocery store, park, and heck, even from Izzy's soccer practice. You said yourself that your son brings that bear with him everywhere."

"I don't believe that. I think he was in my house. What scares the hell out of me is that my son was probably asleep in his *bed* when this guy took the bear from him. That scares me to death, Charles. Gives me nightmares."

"Sheesh, I'd have them too, buddy. What did the detective say?"

"Same thing, different day."

"You're a lawyer; what do you expect?"

"Seems like that would give a guy an advantage."

"No, it's been my experience that lawyering is a disadvantage with most of society, but heck, when anyone needs us, they call."

"And we answer," Todd said, before taking another swig of his drink.

"It's our cross to bear."

They both raised their glasses to that. Charlie wasn't like the other lawyers Todd knew. He was a brilliant lawyer, but he was like someone you'd also find as the owner of a successful hardware store. Most people were often surprised to find out that he was a lawyer if they didn't already know. Perhaps that's what Todd liked about him. He wasn't normal, or possibly in this case he was too normal. Whatever the case, Todd could relate to him. He and Charlie weren't close, but he was the closest friend Todd had next to Vivienne.

Todd slid from his barstool. "I've gotta run."

"Sure you're OK to drive?"

Todd laughed. "It would take more than one bourbon to put me under. Hell, I need more. *Sufficiently numb* is a goal I can't afford right now though."

Charlie smiled. "Bide your time, Todd. This guy will hang himself soon enough. Sure, keep the family safe, but wait him out. Don't move the family again or do anything drastic. This is how he wins, by disrupting you and making your life hell. He's a bully, and we don't give in to bullies."

Todd nodded, tossed a few bills on the bar, and left.

Charlie was right of course, but in the end, biding time depended on the bully.

❦ 38 ❦

P resent
    Seattle, Washington

"I SUSPECT THIS WASN'T SOME RANDOM BREAK-IN, MRS.
Mathis," Detective Glenn said.

"What do you mean?" Vivienne asked. Her daughter sat with
her in a private meeting room at the end of the hall where her son
was fighting for consciousness. He'd failed to wake up after
surgery in the appropriate window, and they were getting a little
nervous. Nurses were avoiding eye contact now, and Vivienne
took that as a bad sign.

The detective wiped his brow and took a deep breath. Vivienne was a mother, and to her that action looked guilty. He was
sweating. Whatever this detective was about to say, he felt
responsible for something. Some part of this he held guilt for, but
what part and why?

"We, ah, dusted for fingerprints, and we had a match."

Isabel looked confused. "Well, that's great. Did you pick him up?"

Detective Glenn shook his head. "No. We are not aware of his current location."

"But you just said you had a match. That means this guy's been in trouble before, so you'd have his location, right?" Her voice was rising slowly.

Vivienne placed her hand on her daughter's to calm her down. The officer was trying to tell them something, and this was only part of the story, she suspected.

He nodded. "True, we should have his location since he's an ex-convict and he's only been recently released, but he's not at the given halfway house that he was assigned to, and no one has seen him since his release apparently. Look, I've got a lot to tell you. I'm not certain how much of this you already know." He looked at Vivienne for recognition.

She stared at him blankly.

"Mrs. Mathis, I have reason to believe that your husband's death was also caused by this same individual."

Every hair on the back of Vivienne's neck and arms rose to attention.

Isabel yelled, "What!" in disbelief. "Dad's death was reported as an accident by a hit-and-run driver."

Vivienne flashed on her husband's mangled body in the morgue. Lying there on a steel table. His eyes shut forever. "I don't understand."

The officer ignored Isabel but responded to Vivienne. "Mrs. Mathis, were you aware of your husband's problems with an individual sending him threats?"

"No." She shook her head. "When?"

He shook his head. "Mr. Mathis came to me back in 1987. Do you recall him having any problems at that time?"

"That's the year Isabel was born. We lived over on Westler then. No, I mean Todd's always been a little overprotective. We've never had our home broken into before though."

"Not that you know of?"

She shook her head.

"OK, well he received a threat in the mail by an unknown individual at that time. We didn't know who the perpetrator was then. There was nothing to go by. A letter appeared in your home mail, along with photographs of you, threatening your life. Your husband took the threat quite seriously at the time."

She couldn't believe it. "Photographs? Of me? I don't remember anything like that. He'd never mentioned it."

"Mom, Brian told me that Dad had mentioned something to him once. That he was concerned for your safety, but he never said why. Could this be it?"

Vivienne was stricken. "I never knew anything about that. Why didn't you tell me?" Vivienne asked.

"I didn't think it was a big deal at the time," Isabel said. "Now, it makes perfect sense."

"In the pictures, you were removing groceries from the car and the other was of you at the grocery store itself. That's not all. Then he came by around 1987 and brought me another envelope that he'd received in the mail again. This time it was your hair clip." He looked into his file again for the description. "A tortoise-shell heirloom hair clip. We released it to your husband after a while. He'd said it was a family keepsake."

Vivienne's hand immediately went to the back of her head. She unclipped the clasp and brought it forward as her hair cascaded down around her face. "Is this the one?"

He looked from her to her opened hand with the clip laying unlatched upon it like some large brown cricket. "I suppose it could be that one. Do you remember losing that item sometime around then?"

"Yes, I do. It's an heirloom from my grandmother. I wear it all the time. It went missing for about a month." Her voice was soft as her eyes glazed over, remembering the scene. "Todd said he'd found it in the backyard. We were so busy then with a newborn. I never understood how it ended up in the backyard."

"Todd received this in his office mail with no return address. He felt it was related to the threatening letter. Which to him meant someone had been in your house to take the item."

"That's when he moved us suddenly. I remember that. All of a sudden he'd found the Lake Union house, and we were selling our old home." Then something terrible came to her. She sucked in her breath and held her hands to her mouth. She looked to Isabel. "The family who bought our house...a year later there was a house fire and the mother died. Is that related? Could he have done that too?"

Detective Glenn's face was ashen. "I wasn't aware of that. I'll look into it." He made notes on his pad.

Isabel spoke up then. "Are you telling me some ex-convict threatened my father for over *twenty years?*" Her anger was blatantly apparent. "And you didn't *do* anything about it?"

Vivienne cut in before the detective could respond. "I don't think he's done explaining to us the whole story, Isabel. Let him finish."

Detective Glynn nodded and avoided eye contact when he began. "Then in 1989, your son was missing a teddy bear." He lifted a large plastic bag containing a padded manila envelope from beside him and opened it up. He pulled out a small stuffed bear with a red-and-green felt scarf about its neck.

"Oh my God!" Vivienne shivered and whispered, "He was inside the house on Lake Union then?" She stared at him with fear, picturing this assailant standing over her young son in his toddler bed at night, pulling the bear from his clasped arms.

"Again, we don't know that he ever entered your house. He could have taken the bear from him in a store or at school. That's what my old notes said. I've been through them all before I came over."

"It sounds to me like you've made a lot of excuses," Isabel said.

"Look, your dad was an attorney. Attorneys receive threats all the time. It was part of his job. He knew that."

"That doesn't give you a pass to shirk your job, sir. He has the same rights you do. He gave you this evidence. Evidence you then ignored. Now, my father is dead, and my brother is lying in a hospital bed down the hall fighting for his life!" She was screaming. "My God, this is why, Mom. This was why he was so crazy protective of you all these years. It all makes sense." She turned a pleading look to her mother, begging to make her see the logic.

Detective Glynn packed up the evidence, his face nearing the color of a sudden sunburn.

"Wait." Vivienne placed her arm on his shoulder. "You said you have a match on the fingerprints. Who? Who's doing this to us?" Vivienne pleaded.

The detective stood. He swallowed hard. His voice betrayed his anger. "We haven't yet linked him directly to your father's accident, but the prints we lifted from your house for the break-in...his name is Eugene Reynolds. And Eugene Reynolds is the cousin of the man who we identified on the camera as being the driver of the car that ran down your husband."

Vivienne stood, shocked with this revelation. Isabel began to speak, but Vivienne spoke over her.

"Was he a client of Todd's? How did he know my husband?"

"He was never a client, ma'am. That's why we had such a hard time trying to find out who would want to harm your family. He was a fraudulent claimant on a benzene case. Your husband defended the oil company out of Nebraska. This guy came along and tried to file an exposure suit but never worked the days the workers cleaned out the benzene tanks. He committed fraud, and the judge gave him five years in prison. And he would have only served two of those years with good behavior had he not committed aggravated murder while in prison, so he ended up serving a lot more time."

Isabel ventured a question, her tone still clipped. "How could he have committed these crimes if he was in prison?"

"He didn't. We suspect he never sent the letter or stole the hair clip or the bear. We suspect he had surrogates commit the crimes for him, possibly the cousin that hit your father. That's why this has been so difficult. The envelopes were mailed by someone else outside of prison. He had photographs of you with the original threatening letter, but he never took them. Someone else did this for him."

He looked at Isabel. "I haven't been ignoring this. It's been a tough case to prove. Honestly, we thought he'd died or moved on because nothing has happened in several years, as far as we know. Most people don't hold grudges for over twenty years."

"How can you tie him to all of this when all you have are the current prints from the break-in?" Vivienne asked.

"Because we ran the prints from your hair clip as well as the envelope, and they belong to his cousin, whose body we found murdered only last month—stabbed to death. His prints were never in the system until we took them off his corpse. He never had a record."

"So this guy, Eugene Reynolds, he's crazy, isn't he? That's what you're saying. He's got it in for my family because he feels my father kept him from hitting it big over twenty years ago?"

"Yes, I believe that's the motive. And we don't have him in custody yet. That's a problem. I'd advise you to find another place to stay for a few days. We'll find him, Mrs. Mathis."

He handed them his card and let them know to contact him anytime, day or night. Something about the detective made Vivienne feel sorry for him. Something got past him all those years ago when her husband went to him for help. Now he was paying for it.

And yet, so did Todd. He'd paid dearly in stress over his family's safety. She'd never understand why he didn't tell her to begin with. But then again, she knew her husband. He'd had a terrible childhood and wanted nothing more than to have a happy home life. That was his goal over all else. He'd protected her and the children from everything. Even if that meant he had to shoulder the demons that tortured him solely alone. Where he couldn't protect his mother from his father, he damn sure would protect them from any harm. But to Vivienne, it was a burden too hard to bear alone.

✣ 39 ✣

P ast
Lake Union, Washington

TODD DROVE UP THE DRIVEWAY OF HIS LAKE UNION HOME that night. Vivienne had the kids out in the front yard playing while she planted bright-red geraniums along the walkway. It was Friday, and he'd had a long week. The added personal stress wasn't helping, but he tried to put it all behind him when he stepped out of the car. That was his routine. Home was home, and nothing he did would affect his family. He'd never bring that stuff home to harm them, ever, no matter what.

"Hi, honey." Vivienne waved as the children ran up to him and into his arms. Brian held onto his leg as he stood and lifted Isabel high into the hair. She squealed. "Again, Daddy!" He tossed her higher still and then he let her down to the ground gently. Then it was Brian's turn, and with a delightful cry from his son, he lifted him into the air. Todd was near exhaustion, but he loved to make them laugh and smile. He always wanted his entrance home to be met with glee instead of trepidation as he'd felt when his father arrived home each day.

"How was your day?" Vivienne asked as she took off her dirty gardening gloves.

He kissed her cheek. "It's better now," he said. He'd always hated that question, but he knew Vivienne meant it out of routine respect. She didn't want to him to recount his entire dreadful day with her.

He led the kids inside the house and washed his hands while he talked with them about their day at school so that Vivienne could finish planting the flowers without having to keep a constant eye on the children.

When she finished planting, Todd walked out to see the final effect. The walkway was lined with red like a welcome showcase to their front door, an unmistakable path. It bothered him some-how, but he neglected to voice his opinion. The flowers were a charming addition to the front yard.

Then when he returned inside, a casserole simmered in the oven. Vivienne began to prepare a salad, and the children set the table. He jumped in where he could, and they sat down together as a family at the table. They passed the plates, filling each with a good quantity. He looked around him. A boy and a girl and a lovely wife of his very own. He was the luckiest man in the world and acknowledged that fact to himself each day. He'd die for each of them, so the stress from the outside world he left to drift away. After taking a big breath, he squeezed his wife's hand. He was home for the weekend with his family in that moment. Nothing else would affect him. He kept all demons on the other side of the red path that led to the front door.

❊ 40 ❊

P resent
Seattle, Washington

"EUGENE REYNOLDS?" ISABEL SAID QUIZZICALLY, SITTING IN A chair next to her unconscious brother. Machines beeped softly in the background. Vivienne leaned her weight against the metal windowpane spanning from the floor to the ceiling while peering outside for the many answers she sought.

"Did Daddy ever mention that name before, Mom?"

She shook her head. "No, not once. He never talked about work at home." And yet she knew Todd would have killed the man with his bare hands if he'd revealed himself, knowing what she knew now. It was one thing to say that you knew your husband *could* kill a man; it was another to know that he *would have* killed him had he had the chance. Without a doubt Vivienne knew Todd was in the latter group. Todd not only needed to know his family was safe but he demanded that safety.

This individual tortured her husband like a coward, with an

invisible hand. Todd was not a man to be tortured. He was not a man anyone wanted to face in court either. Todd was a man to be feared. Only a coward could torture him from afar. A coward without a face—that was the only way he could get away with hurting Todd.

Though there was one thing Vivienne was angry at Todd for. If he were standing in front of her now, she'd have let him have it. Rarely had they argued, but this, this was enough for her to throw the biggest fit of all time. He'd kept this pain from her and suffered through it alone. Even though he'd done everything to keep her from knowing so that they could have a comfortable family life, this, *this* wasn't fair. It wasn't fair of him to not share this pain with her. She felt deceived as if he'd had an affair and betrayed her, and she was only finding out about it now. Actually, something like that might have been easier to take than this, she imagined. Todd had betrayed her trust in the worst of ways. He'd lived a lie. They were in danger...her children were in danger, and he'd never confided this threat with her, never once.

Instead, he made her question his sanity when she protested and needed to have some alone time. He would have fitted her body with a tracking device if it were legal. They'd even joked about it once, but now she knew the desire was real.

He had the security people swarm all over their house and installed cameras without asking her about it first, claiming home break-ins in the area as his rationale. She now knew that it was related to this. *How could he keep this from me?*

The answer to that was easily defined now. Only Todd was the provider. He felt it was his job, his burden to bear.

"Mom?" Isabel said again.

Vivienne had not heard her the first time.

She turned from the window. At first she thought Isabel had another rhetorical question she could not answer, but it wasn't that. When she turned to Isabel on the other side of Brian's hospital bed, she was staring at Brian's face. Reluctant to break the trance. His eyes were fluttering open.

Vivienne quickly took steps toward him, taking his other hand. "Go get the nurse, Izzy."

Vivienne locked eyes with her son, never leaving them as Isabel's feet hit the tiles, and soon other footsteps could be heard rushing quickly to the room. Still, Vivienne held her son's sight. She smiled at him. He looked at her questioningly. "You're going to be all right, son." She brushed away the hair from his forehead as the nurses came in and busily checked his vitals. It had taken too long for him to come to after surgery, and he was in obvious pain and confusion, and he couldn't talk with the tubes down his throat.

His eyes searched for Katherine and then back to his mother. She'd guessed what he needed. "Katherine just stepped out to check on the girls. She'll be right back, and she'll be so relieved you've come back to us." She smiled, and another tear fell onto his light-blue hospital gown, staining a darker circle in the material.

He'd tried to nod that he understood, but even that was difficult. She was certain he would have a lot of questions after they removed the ventilator. No doubt he was confused as to what had happened and why he was in the hospital at all. He may not even remember the event, but she wanted to know if Brian had gotten a good look at this Eugene Reynolds, the person who'd had her husband killed, shot her son in her home, and privately tortured their family for all the years of their lives.

❦ 41 ❦

P resent
   Seattle, Washington

ONCE KATHERINE RETURNED, VIVIENNE AND ISABEL GAVE them some time to themselves. They went back to the hotel to relax for the night, thankful that Brian was out of danger, as the doctor assessed his condition, and was expected to recover fully.

"The detective said not to go back to the house for a few days. What are we going to do?" Isabel said.

Vivienne nodded, though her mind was elsewhere. She removed her scarf and laid back on the hotel bed. Feeling relieved for the first time in days, she was now trying to figure out what came next.

"Mom, I think we should sell the house after what's happened. They may never catch this guy."

Vivienne heard her daughter's words, but she wasn't thinking along those lines at all.

She smiled at her daughter. "Isabel, I think it's time for you to return soon. Brian's going to recover, and I'm fine. The police are watching the house. What's best is that we get on with our lives. We can't let this deter us from our goals in life, or he wins."

"But, Mom, Detective Glynn linked this guy to Dad's death too. I can't leave you here knowing that."

"Isabel, your brother is going to recover. The investigators are on his trail. They'll let us know whatever they find out. There's nothing we can do about it. There's no use for you to stay and miss work, and what about Armand? I know he's worried about you."

Her daughter's eyes filled with tears. "I can't leave you, Mom."

Vivienne sat up. "I'm not going to let this creep destroy our lives, darling. No. I won't let him keep you from doing the things you love. Your father would never have wanted that. Isabel, go back to Paris, live, love, and do what you've always done. Don't despair over the things we cannot control. You have important work waiting for you. I've seen the stress when your boss texts you. I know you have left your responsibilities there. You've got to go back now that your brother is recovering. I'll keep you informed of the investigation. There's really nothing you can do here anyway."

Isabel reluctantly agreed and booked her flight to leave Seattle in two days' time. She'd admitted that her employer was getting more and more frustrated with her absence, even though she'd had a family crisis going on.

The next morning, she met with the detective again as they questioned Brian in the hospital room. Isabel took Katherine for a coffee run.

"I apologize in advance for what has happened to your family, Mr. Mathis."

Brian nodded curtly. Vivienne took a seat on his left side as the detective sat on his right, near the window. "What is it you want to ask me? The meds they give me are making me really sleepy, and they just gave me one, so we don't have much time."

The detective smirked. "I know how that goes. I was in your position last year, similar injury. You'll be yourself in no time. The first week is the worst."

The conversation seemed to settle her son a little, though she noticed he had a hold of the sheets with his hand on her side, twisting the fabric a little every now and then. That was something he used to do as a child when he was in trouble. She diverted her eyes back to the conversation as the detective took out a notepad and pen.

"Well, let's begin. Do you remember anything about that morning?"

Again, Brian was twisting the sheets next to his outer thigh. The detective didn't notice.

"I remember walking from the car and using my key to get into the door. I stepped into the foyer and walked down the hall toward the kitchen. I remember hearing someone near Mom's room...you know, like someone was putting away laundry or something. Then I backed up and peered down the hall, and I thought maybe it was one of the security guards, but then I remembered there were no other cars in the driveway. I said, 'Hello?' No one answered. I was about to head for the hall when I saw someone standing there and then I heard a loud pop. I had no idea I'd been shot. I ducked, and my hands went to my ears automatically. It was deafening. I looked down the hall again. He raised his arm again, with a pistol in his hand, and I ran for the door. It was all in slow motion. I ran for my car and took off. I was well down the highway before I realized there was blood all over me. I never felt the pain until I saw the blood staining my shirt."

The detective wrote quickly. He looked at Brian then and asked, "Did you get a good look at the guy? Could you describe him to me?"

Brian shook his head and twisted the sheets into his tight fist. "You know, I've been trying to focus on the guy's face, but I don't think I actually saw his face, only the gun. There were no lights on, and it was dark in the hallway."

"Did you get a look at the gun? Do you know what it was?"

"I don't know gun models. It was a handgun. I was only focused on avoiding the barrel end," he joked.

"Yeah, I bet," the detective said. "But you're certain it was a male."

Brian nodded. "Yes. That I'm certain of."

Vivienne cut in quickly. "Brian, could it be the same man you saw who was watching the house after the funeral?"

Brian shook his head. "I really couldn't describe that guy either. He was up on the trail behind some trees. They could have been the same, but honestly, they probably weren't."

The detective noted their conversation and then asked, "What was the height and weight of the shooter?"

"Maybe five eleven, maybe one sixty-five."

"Color of hair?"

"I can only say it wasn't blond, I think. I'm sorry, my memory is really fuzzy. I don't think I'm giving you much to go on."

"Your sister mentioned that your father confided in you about someone trying to harm your mother? What do you know about that?"

Vivienne watched as her son swallowed hard and looked at her as if he'd done something wrong. Brian didn't look at the detective. He stared into his mother's eyes instead. She was waiting for this. That's why she wanted to be there for the interview with her son.

He twisted the sheets again. "Mom, years ago, Dad said that if anything were to ever happen to him that I needed to protect you. He'd had a few drinks, which wasn't like him...ever. I tried to ask him why, but he wouldn't say. I always suspected that there was more to the story. I think this was it. I'm sorry I never told you. I thought Dad had one too many. I'd never seen him have more than one drink at a time before or since that night at Fred's."

She clenched the hand that held the sheet tightly before, releasing his tension. "Son, I would expect you to be loyal to your father. You had no way of knowing this is what he meant. None of us did. I wish he'd told us."

"I just feel awful having kept it from you."

"How were you to know?"

The detective fished a picture out of a folder of several head-shots of individuals and showed the collage to Brian. "Can you look at these people and point him out to me?"

Brian studied the photos for a while and then shook his head. "No, I...like I said, I can only give you a vague description. Look, Katherine filled me in on the conversation you had with my mom and sister. You believe whoever did this might also be responsible for my father's death?" Brian's voice rose.

"We aren't certain of anything right now. We have to treat your attack as a separate incident. We have however, discovered that the driver of the car that hit your father was identified as the cousin of the guy whose prints were left at your mom's house."

"Katherine mentioned that. Did you pick up him up?"

"We can't. He's dead. I told your mom we found him last month with multiple stab wounds in a known drug house."

"What about the prints you lifted from the house? Did he leave the firearm?"

"We found three matching prints in various parts of the house." He looked through his notes. "One was on the garage side-door locks, one on the laundry-room light-switch plate, and one on the studio light-switch plate. Seems like he was in there for a while too. He didn't leave the gun."

Vivienne found it creepy that he might have been gazing at her artwork.

"How did he get inside?"

"We still don't know. There's no sign of forced entry. Maybe he has a key and let himself in. He certainly didn't know the security code because that's what alerted them. The local police did do a drive by at eleven fifty-four that night, but they found nothing and said it was probably a malfunction."

The detective peeked quickly at Vivienne sitting silently and watching the interview.

"Your father foiled this guy's attempt to make big money a long time ago, and apparently he's held a grudge. His attempt to cash in on a faked benzene claim was well before you were born. We believe he is the one that threatened your mother's life and stole your teddy bear when you were a toddler."

Brian suddenly looked concerned. "Wait what? Katherine told me about the lost hair clip but not about a bear." He looked from his mother to the officer again. "Uh, who the hell took my bear?" He sort of smirked at the reference to his childhood toy.

The detective chuckled. "Well, years ago, your dad came to me with this envelope, and inside was a bear you had lost as a toddler."

"Oh geez." Brian pulled his hand down his face, noting he had started growing a beard in his unconscious state. "Poor Dad," Brian said, after letting the implications set in. "So Dad had to deal with this all these years, and he never told anyone...but me, in a way?" He'd directed the question to his mother.

Vivienne looked to the detective. "He told him," she said, nodding her head in his direction.

Brian looked to the detective again. "And there was *nothing* you could do about this?"

The detective shook his head. "No. We lifted prints from the clip, but we had no match in the database for those prints. Then your father died in what looked like a tragic hit-and-run. Then, we identified the driver of the car through surveillance equipment. And when we found the cousin's body and we ran his prints, this case popped up when we dug into his family. At first I thought we'd finally found our guy, but that's not the case. Now we know it was his cousin, and he was the one sending these threats to your family all this time through his surrogate."

The detective looked guilty. "When the prints were found on the dead body, the morgue ran those, and they found the old match on the clip. We finally had a name with a print. We compared them with face recognition as the driver of the car."

"And you think he killed his own cousin?" Brian asked.

"We don't know. It looks that way. At least that's what the wife claims."

"And you have no idea where this Eugene Reynolds is today?"

"I really wish I did."

"Me too," Brian said, and wondered why his father didn't tell him more. Then he knew: he'd never wanted this burden to carry over to his son. He was silent for a moment in thought. "So it wasn't the cousin who shot me. It was Reynolds. He was in our house this time." He turned to his mother suddenly and tried to sit up but recoiled in pain. "Mom, you can't go home. This guy is out there, and he's nuts."

She smiled, but Detective Glynn said, "The police are surveilling the house, and I'm certain he's long gone by now. Your mother is safe to go home now."

Brian didn't look convinced, even though the detective was reassuring him.

❄ 42 ❄

P ast
Seattle, Washington

TODD STARED OUT THE OPEN WINDOW OF HIS OFFICE WITH THE
lights off, and with one leg crossed over the other, he leaned back
into his leather chair with his left arm on the armrest and the
other propped under his chin. For some reason, he thought best
in this position.

His office assistant came through the door after a courteous
knock. She noted the darkened room and flipped on the light.
"Good afternoon, Mr. Mathis. Your client Sabastian Godfrey is
here to see you."

Todd dropped his leg, sat up, and turned himself toward his
desk, which was piled high with letters and on top, another
manila envelope overstuffed with something tangible inside. He
shoved the mail into his top drawer and picked up the package
with two fingers and hovered it over the wastebin near his desk.

He didn't know what was inside the unmarked manila envelope, and he didn't care anymore. If he cared, then his aggressor won, and he wasn't going to let him win. He watched as the package hit the bottom of the trash basin.

"Send him in," he said to his assistant.

He'd thought about the envelope for a long time and decided it didn't matter what was inside the packages anymore. He wouldn't report them to the detective any longer. He wouldn't worry about them either. He would discard them, and that was that.

After he spoke with his new client, it was time to head home for the day. He stood at his office door, knowing the night cleaning crew would empty his trash. He turned off his office light and stopped to make sure he felt the same about the package. This way, he wouldn't let the perpetrator have his fun, because it seemed to be a game to him, and Todd was no longer playing the game. He flipped the light off once again and softly closed the door and headed home.

❧ 43 ❧

P resent
Seattle, Washington

ISABEL HUGGED HER MOTHER. THEY'D ARGUED AGAIN THE night before, though Vivienne remained convinced that Isabel should leave as soon as possible. There were things she needed to do, and having Isabel out of the picture, safely in France and out of danger, was her goal.

If she could send Brian and Katherine and the girls away too, she would have arranged that as well, but Brian had work to do, and he was being released from the hospital in the next day.

Now, she was once again making her way to the airport with Isabel early in the morning to see her off. They barely spoke as the cab pulled up in front of the airport.

Vivienne continued to say over and over to herself...*bide your time*. In her mind she already knew what she was going to do... down to the last minute detail. The plan began to formulate as soon as she saw her son lying there in the hospital fighting for his life. Then when the detective voiced the link between the driver of the car that killed her husband and Brian's shooter, her mind worked overtime. There was a menace to be dealt with.

Isabel sat there for a moment, staring straight ahead. "I don't know why you had to come with me, mom. I could have come by myself."

"It's no bother, Izzy. I wanted to see for myself that you got here safely."

"I should be the one worried about you. I don't want to leave you here with a killer, someone who may have murdered my father, out on the loose. He might come after you, Mom." Isabel's voice faltered in her last plea.

What Vivienne didn't say was, "That's what I'm banking on." Instead she said, "The police are watching the house. I've had more security installed. There's nothing to worry about. I'm not worried. I'll call you more often and let you know how the investigation is progressing, Izzy. Everything's going to be fine. You'll see."

❧ 44 ☙

P ast
Lake Union, Washington

"BYE, DAD," BRIAN CALLED FROM THE DRIVEWAY AS HE LEFT for school, driving himself for the first week ever.

"Bye, son, be careful around these narrow roads," Todd said as he buckled on his bike helmet.

Vivienne kissed him good-bye. And he waited for her to retreat back inside and turn the deadbolt before he would leave. He was aware of how it looked, but he didn't care. For some reason if she didn't turn that lock and set the alarm before he left, it drove him crazy, and he would end up worried about her all day.

Visions of coming home and finding her mangled body and blood all over the house haunted him, or worse yet, that she simply disappeared. The visions were relentless. He'd taken up biking to help combat his anxiety.

Now that the kids were old enough to drive themselves every-where, Vivienne stayed home more, and at times he worried that

her predictable routine was easier for the "package man" to inter-
cept her. "Stop," he told himself and pedaled faster.

It had rained that morning, and dirty wet spray from the road
flicked up into his clothing. Though that was nothing new for
him, biking the city streets of Seattle. Thankfully, he was able to
utilize the showers and extra apparel at work.

His mind kept wandering to the *package man*. It always did
when he hadn't received one in a few months. He knew another
was on its way soon. Every year at least three or four showed up
almost like clockwork. It had been at least three months since the
last one appeared, and he never opened them anymore, so he had
no idea what might have been inside.

Things went missing in the household all the time. Sometimes
they were found, and others never showed up again. He couldn't
help but guess if that was the item taken and bestowed inside a
package he'd never open. He told himself it didn't matter. It
would eventually stop. Either the guy would drop dead out of
pure malice or he'd be caught doing the same thing to someone
else. That's what he told himself...over and over.

❅ 45 ❅

P resent
    Lake Union, Washington

THE RAIN HAD COME AND GONE, AND VIVIENNE WAS OUT
walking after she'd cleaned house for the morning. It was Saturday
after all, and she'd worked all week at the art studio covering for a
sick coworker. She'd worked even harder at home until late at
night. She'd even started another class after the teacher on maternity leave had returned. She found she enjoyed coming and going.
And as of last night, she was ready for him. She was ready...for
anything.

Except that as she turned the corner on her way back to her
house, she spotted a car out front. Brian's car slid into her driveway. That was a problem. "Dang, not now."

Vivienne picked up her pace. She smiled and waved at Brian
when he noticed her walking their way.

"Hi, Mom."

"Son, what are you doing here?" she smiled but seriously she wanted to know why he hadn't called first. Then she noticed Katherine and the girls also in the car.

"We were out looking at furniture and somehow found ourselves closer to you. Thought we'd pop in."

"Oh, well...the house is a mess right now. I've got paint and supplies scattered everywhere. How about we go out to dinner?" Before he could say anything, she quickly said, "I'll grab my purse and be right back."

She ran inside and hoped he didn't follow her. She found her purse in the hall closet and changed her shoes quickly before stepping back out, resetting the trap on her way.

She slid into the backseat with the girls and greeted them with kisses and smiles. "I've missed seeing you little ladies."

Brian peeked at her with some suspicion through the rearview mirror. He knew something was up, and she was going to have to play this down to the very last molecule because her son knew her best of all. She'd have a hard time hiding her plan from him. This was how it would have to be though, and she was prepared to temporarily sever ties with her children if it came to that, just so she could end this nightmare.

"Mom, is everything all right? How has work been? I feel like I never see you anymore," he said once they were seated in a nearby steak house with loud music and families all around them.

"Oh, I'm sorry, son. Yes, everything's fine. I've just been busy. Since I'm closer to your side of town when I'm working, how about I come over or meet you guys for dinner to catch up every now and then?" She figured a preemptive strike might work.

Katherine was the first to speak. "That's a wonderful idea. That way we can stay in touch better. You know how Brian worries about you."

"Oh, no need to worry about me. I'm just busy," Vivienne said, though the lingering look on her son's face said that he suspected something more. There was more but she wasn't going to let him in on it. She needed to keep them away from her true intentions.

"I'm going to take the girls to the bathroom to wash their hands before dinner," Katherine said, and led the children away.

Vivienne knew it was a ploy for Brian to ask her questions she'd rather not answer. They never talked about the shooting in front of the girls.

"Any news from the detective?" Brian asked.

Vivienne shook her head after she'd taken a drink of water. "No, have you heard from him?"

Brian too shook his head. "No. I'm sure this is what Dad went through with him as well. They drop this all on us, and then that's it. You don't hear from them forever until something else happens."

"Well, thank God you're doing better," Vivienne said.

"Yes, well. I've got to say if this guy had anything to do with Dad's death...I'm going to haunt the hell out of him when he's caught."

She could see Brian's blood pressure rise with his statement. She suspected he was keeping his rage just undetected. He was so much like his father.

Vivienne knew it would never come to that. She had no intention of anyone ever finding out who this guy was. She owed him. She owed him for so much, and she was going to make sure he got it.

✤ 46 ✤

P resent
Lake Union, Washington

ONE EVENING TWO MONTHS LATER, VIVIENNE RECEIVED A CALL
from her son as she tied the boat up. "Mom, I'm not comfortable
with the way things are going. There's something wrong and
you're not telling me what's going on. I can feel it."

"Brian, everything's fine now. I don't know what you mean.
I've been awfully busy with work lately."

"Why don't you want us coming over to the house anymore? It
doesn't make sense. You wanted us to take over the property
there for a while. Now you always make excuses to meet us somewhere else. Are you afraid I'm scared or something? Because
that's where I was shot?"

"The assault certainly crossed my mind. But no, I'm not
actively trying to keep you from coming over. Why don't you and
the girls come over this weekend for dinner? We can talk about

the house then. I wasn't sure if you were still interested in taking the house after what happened here."

There was a pause in the conversation. She'd held him off as long as she could, and now that things were taken care of, she could relax her guard, finally.

"OK." He sounded tentative. "We'll come over Saturday. Do you want us to bring anything?"

Vivienne smiled to herself. "No, you don't need to bring anything. I've got everything here."

"OK, Mom. I love you. See you then."

When he ended the call, Vivienne relaxed. The tension in her body drifted away. Everything was fine, finally, after so much time and so much pain.

The next morning Vivienne called Isabel in Paris, where it was dinner time.

"Hi, Mom. How's the investigation going?"

"What? Oh. I have no idea. I've not heard from the detective in weeks now. No, I was calling because I thought now that things have settled down, we might try that visit again. Maybe next month?"

"Really? You're ready to come back? I never thought you'd leave again after what happened last time. Things are going well?"

"Yes, everything is fine."

"You're not concerned about that guy breaking in again?"

"No, I think the new security equipment is in place, and the police take extra trips by every now and then. I say we get on with our lives. Don't you think we've given him enough of our time? Besides, someone like that is bound to meet a bigger, badder guy that will take him out."

"Well...was there anything else linking him to Daddy's death?"

"No. I don't think they will ever know for sure. And he's probably long gone by now. I doubt we'll be hearing from the detective for some time. Unless they accidentally find something."

"OK, well, if you're sure."

"I'm confident I don't want to waste any more of my time on this. I want to see you and spend more time in Paris. And I'd like to meet Armand."

Isabel laughed. "I'm so happy you feel that way. Sounds like the same attitude Daddy had, though I wish he'd told us. We could have tried to prevent it."

"Isabel, we would have been living in a prison of our own making then. So much worse than what your Dad felt he was doing to protect me."

"You've thought about this a lot. You're right; we should move on."

Present
Seattle, Washington

ON SATURDAY, VIVIENNE SET THE TABLE IN THE FORMAL dining room. The weather was colder, and she made sure the heat was set to a comfortable temperature inside. Brian and his family arrived around noon. They'd planned to spend the day together, and Brian was going to help Vivienne do the winter maintenance on the boat.

When Katherine came through the door bearing a salad to go with their planned last-barbecue-of-the-year, she smiled but avoided eye contact with her mother-in-law. Vivienne knew something was up. And that something was very good news indeed. She could always tell when Katherine was pregnant before—they'd even mentioned contemplating the third child—and she wondered how long they were going to wait before telling her the deed was done.

She'd noticed a spark in Katherine not too long after Brian

was shot, and she suspected that incident probably brought the two together in ways no young married couple should have to face. Having the prospect of losing your loved one so early in married life shook them both.

They would certainly need the house with a third child on the way, because their three-bedroom wouldn't suffice for much longer. She was happy that now she could pass on the house to them safely.

They sat around the patio table bundled in sweaters, drinking hot cocoa, eating, and laughing at the children's antics. Vivienne picked up the dirty dishes and walked them into the kitchen. Brian grabbed several as well and said, "Let me help you, Mom." They quickly washed them while chatting and watching the girls through the kitchen window run around on the grass of the backyard, the leaves being tossed around by the wind. They were happy...finally. Laughing the way a family should.

"Oh, hey, I want to show you something," she said to Brian. He followed her back down the hall to her studio.

Brian stopped and waved a hand in front of his face. "Whew, what is that smell?"

"Oh, I repainted the laundry room. The paint is still gassing off, I guess." She flipped on the air vent.

He peeked inside the laundry room and noticed the new green wall color. "I like it," he said. "You got new appliances?"

"It's called Frog Belly Green. Yeah, the washer was leaking, and when I called about the warranty, it was expired, so I went down to get a new one. This set was on sale, so I decided to replace them both at the same time. It was pretty easy. They took the old ones away and set it up for me. I painted the walls between deliveries. The blue was just so dated."

He nodded his head and then they continued to the room she used as a studio. She led him to her current painting sitting on the easel in front of the opened window. Her latest canvas sat there filled with bright colors. The dark shadows contrasting to the glorious sunset over the waves of Puget Sound.

"Wow, you're painting again. Is that the sound?"

"Yes, it's beautiful out there in the evening this time of year."

Then Sybil called for her from the back door. "Grandma?"

"Oh, excuse me," she said, and left him staring at the painting.

He stood there for a long time noticing how the brilliant twilight was above the sea and how in the bottom depths there was something there, dark and hidden beneath the cove.

Brian walked away from the painting and stepped across the hall, staring into the dark Frog Belly–green laundry room again. He turned off the vent fan and stood there silently peering inside a minute longer. He finally nodded his head as if reasoning something through to himself. Something never said.

❦ 48 ❦

P resent
Seattle, Washington

VIVIENNE VISITED TODD'S GRAVE FOR THE FIRST TIME IN
several weeks. She'd come after Brian was attacked. She'd come
while debating her plan. Little moments she stole from her daily
life to share them with Todd. She was angry at him for what he
kept from her all those years and had not shared.

Instead, he chose to burden her with an invisible barrier
instead of trusting her with the knowledge. Had she known,
perhaps things would have been different. Perhaps he would still
be alive. Though she couldn't blame him, really. She knew why he
held the misery to himself.

It didn't matter now. She'd ended the nightmare for the both
of them. She knelt at his graveside and pulled out the spent
chrysanthemums she'd brought the time before, now replacing
them with small picks of faux poinsettias. She bent the wire

bottoms of the picks before she pushed them into the stone urn near his headstone.

"Our daughter is to be married soon. I so wish you could be there. And Katherine and Brian are expecting a son this time." She smiled with happy tears spilling down her cheeks. "You don't have to worry about us anymore, Todd. Rest now, my dear. I fed the fishes."

She remembered that evening well, a painting session she would likely never forget.

When she came home from teaching that night, she was finally relieved to find what she'd hoped for all these months. A pest locked inside of her trap. He'd come in the way she'd hoped, through the laundry-room window, the one she left unlocked just for him. The one-way entrance was rigged so that her prey could get inside but could never escape.

The door to the interior was completely sealed, the switch plate removed and covered with a solid plate. He could not have known that from the outside. She'd simply looked through the camera after the alarm signaled her. Then she went into the garage and turned on Todd's car. The garage door remained closed. He'd screamed and yelled for about five minutes, but that was all. The exhaust filtered perfectly through the pipe that she'd fitted to the dryer-hose vent.

He'd banged and clawed the walls when the realization dawned on him, and when she looked through the camera, he was making a mess of the room, violating the washer and dryer, trying to find something, anything, to use to get out his readymade coffin, but she'd already gone through the trouble and removed all likely weapons or tools that he might conceivably try to use to escape her trap. To Vivienne he was like a mouse, a rodent, and nothing more than a menace that she would deal with efficiently.

In a moment's doubt, she wondered if she had the right man. Perhaps it was another burglar? But Eugene Reynolds screamed her name as she walked by. "Vivienne Mathis, I know you're home," he'd said, in a voice that made her skin crawl. She wasn't scared in the least. She never uttered a word. She inched past the sealed laundry-room door and into the attached garage. It *was* him, and she was sure.

After ten minutes, just to be certain, she turned off the car ignition. Five minutes would have done the job proficiently. She'd done the research and knew that was enough time to exterminate the problem. She'd checked the hidden camera once again and saw that he was unconscious on the floor, laying on his side in a fetal position.

Such a misery of a man, having caused so much pain for so many. And having caused her husband a near lifetime of worry, this menace deserved so much worse. She was taking the high road by not torturing him first, as her own father had tortured the man that attacked her mother.

Once she was sure, she opened the door and checked his pulse, or rather the lack of one. Then she opened a cupboard and pulled out a dark-brown leaf tarp. The sturdy handles on the outside came in handy later that evening. The weighted tarp slid easily over the wet, sloped grass down to the dock and into the boat. The whole process took her less than a minute. No one was out that time of day during the week, which was precisely the reason Mr. Reynolds had broken in at that time.

Then, after she'd cleaned her trap for the man, she took her regular evening jaunt in the boat with her painting and a thermos of Earl Gray tea. She waved to the few people she ran into along the way through the locks and out into Puget Sound. Dusk was her favorite time of day.

The sun glazed on the horizon in perfect contrast. She sat on a cushion and painted near a cove. When she was ready for a break, she'd sipped the tea she'd brought along and thanked Todd for always keeping an extra cargo net and anchor on board.

AFTERWORD

I hope you enjoy *The French Wardrobe*. You never know where fiction will take you. I'd set out to write a novel about a grieving widow learning to survive in a new life full of struggles. The story, however, took a different path than I'd intended but one I hope you'll enjoy.

As in all stories, there is a bit of myth combined in fiction along with real facts. Though there is no stylist company named *The Wardrobe*, there is one name *Trunk Club* and my stylist, was the inspiration behind the one in the story. If you're interested in having a stylist, as described, you can contact her here. (This is an affiliate link.)

Before you go!

Sign up for A. R. Shaw's spam-free newsletter for special offers and her latest new releases here AuthorARShaw.com

Follow A. R. Shaw here

Please write a review on Amazon.com; even a quick word about your experience can be helpful to prospective readers.

Click here to write a review.

The author welcomes any comments, feedback, or questions at Annette@AuthorARShaw.com.

ABOUT THE AUTHOR

A. R. Shaw is the bestselling author of the Graham's Resolution and Surrender the Sun series. She served in the United States Air Force Reserves as a Communications Radio Operator and then attended college as a mother of four. She's always written in what little off time she could manage but didn't start publishing her works until 2013.

Now when she isn't writing or spending time with family she enjoys, running, biking and traveling. She conquered the Spartan Sprint Race recently and lives in Ohio with her loyal tabby cat, Henry, and a house full of books.

Made in the USA
San Bernardino, CA
14 January 2019